THE GARDENER'S SECRET

JAMIE CORTLAND

This is a work of fiction. Names, characters, places, and incidents are products of the author's imagination or are used fictitiously and are not to be construed as real. Any resemblance to actual events, locations, organizations, or persons, living or dead, is entirely coincidental.

World Castle Publishing, LLC
Pensacola, Florida
Copyright © Jamie Cortland 2017
Paperback ISBN: 9781629897318
eBook ISBN: 9781629897325
First Edition World Castle Publishing, LLC, July 17, 2017
http://www.worldcastlepublishing.com

Licensing Notes

Cover: Karen Fuller
Editor: Maxine Bringenberg

Chapter 1
Eddie

Eddie drove south on A1A from Delray, glancing occasionally to the oceanfront homes on his left looking for lawns and young women that appeared to need his special brand of TLC. As he slowed down to observe the mansion on his left, a beautiful auburn haired woman, who appeared to be in her early thirties. opened the massive front door and walked down the curved driveway to the bright red Ferrari. Opening the door, she slid into it, turned over the engine, and pulled out of the driveway heading north. Whoever she was, she needed his services. He pulled into the parking lot of the hotel down the road, turned around, and drove north, slowing down long enough to take down the address of her home. Once he'd taken down the address he picked up speed. When he was close enough, he memorized the numbers of the license plate.

When he returned to the small apartment he was renting in Pompano Beach, he booted up his computer. After a thorough search, he discovered that the Giardinis, both partners in JVS Development Company, owned the Ferrari and the home jointly. He watched the home and its two occupants for several days. When the woman left with Mr. Giardini on Friday morning, he followed them to JVS's offices. Several hours later, she left alone to run errands and returned home without her husband. Down the street from her home, he parked in a lot by the intra-coastal and waited for her to step out of her home again. It was not long. When she did, he continued tailing her, hoping that she would go to a department store or to the post office so that he could go into the store and catch a closer glimpse of her, maybe bump into her and even speak with her. But he realized that wasn't going to happen when she returned to the office.

He sighed, satisfied. He'd seen the woman of his dreams and he intended to have her, one way or another.

CHAPTER 2
FLIGHT #1920

A chill snaked up Vince's spine as he boarded flight #1920 to Denver. When he took his seat, he wanted to bolt. He'd never felt like this before on any flight. Why now? Security was more than adequate. He glanced at the other passengers...skiers, businesspersons, women with children, couples on winter vacations; the normal jet load of passengers. Nevertheless, he felt uneasy. Maybe because he'd taken a commercial airline. He usually traveled in the company jet, and never in a winter storm as The Weather Channel had predicted. However, that would not happen, not until they were in the Rockies. Vince forced himself to settle down in his seat. It would be okay, he told himself as he fastened his seat belt.

Once they were in the air, he ordered a double bourbon and water on the rocks. He opened the best-selling mystery novel he'd just purchased at the airport. A few pages into it, he realized he wasn't going to be able to read no matter how compelling the book. Sleeping through the flight would be the best thing. Downing his drink, he dozed off for a couple of minutes. He awoke, jolted by the plane's rapid drop in altitude.

"What happened?" Vince asked the passenger on the other side of the aisle.

"Jeez. I don't know. Maybe we hit an air pocket."

"Damn!" He cursed as the plane hit another rough spot.

"It's going to be bumpy for a while," the pilot announced. "Keep your seat belts on."

The middle-aged woman sitting just next to Vince placed her hand on his forearm. "What do you think is going on?"

"Bad weather, maybe."

She shook her head. "I have a bad feeling about this flight."

Vince took a deep breath. His mouth was dry. He pushed the button to call the hostess, but she didn't respond. Well, one thing about it, if he had just boarded one too many planes, at least he'd made the necessary changes to his will and his trust to include his mistress. Though neither his partners nor Danni knew she existed, his attorney had been well informed.

The plane bumped along, feeling and sounding as though it was falling apart. Several overhead luggage compartments fell open. Oxygen masks dropped down at random. Vince glanced out the window, wishing that he'd never boarded the plane.

"Due to mechanical difficulties, we'll be making an unexpected stop in Albuquerque. We expect to be on the ground approximately forty-five minutes to an hour. Those who wish to stay on board may do so. The rest of you may deplane and reboard later. I'm sorry for the delay, folks, but we'll be on our way again as soon as possible."

"I knew there was something wrong." The woman next to Vince shifted in her seat. "I think it's a lot worse than they're telling us. I'm getting off this plane, and I'm not getting back on, repairs or not."

After a rough landing in Albuquerque, Vince took his briefcase, grabbed his backpack, departed the plane, called Sal to advise him of the delay, and headed toward the cocktail lounge. An hour later, an announcement was made. The parts required to make the repairs weren't available in Albuquerque;

however, the captain assured them that the plane was safe to make the relatively short flight on into Denver, where the parts were available. Those who felt uncomfortable continuing on the flight were given permission to book another... on this airline or on another. If they had checked luggage, they only needed to ask that it be taken off the plane. If the passengers chose to fly another airline, no refunds would be made.

Vince downed his drink while weighing the pros and cons. He could easily stay overnight at one of the airport hotels and fly into Denver the following morning. Still, if the captain felt it was safe to fly this plane on into Denver, then it should be okay. He rose and moved back to the gate to re-board the jet. Handing the agent his boarding card, he walked onto the jet-way carrying his briefcase. Halfway down, he realized he'd forgotten his backpack. He turned, nearly bumping into the passenger behind him.

"Sorry, I forgot something."

The agent who had taken his boarding pass was busy with other passengers and didn't notice him as he left the jet-way. Walking back into the bar, he saw his backpack resting on the floor near the bar stool that he'd been sitting in. He retrieved the backpack, and started back to re-board the plane again.

CHAPTER 3
NOTIFICATION

Sal awaited the arrival of flight #1920 into Denver. It was freezing outside. A winter storm had moved in earlier and it was snowing heavily. Visibility was low even for driving. Streets were icy. He shook his head. *I wouldn't want to fly or land a plane in this. But, at least, it's Denver…not Pitkin County/Aspen Airport.* Surrounded by mountains on three sides, it would be nearly impossible to fly into Aspen tonight. He was glad they had decided to meet in Denver, but Vince's flight was long overdue.

"Flight 1920 from Albuquerque has been delayed until further notice," the person on the loudspeaker announced.

Sal ran his fingers through his hair. *Man, that doesn't sound good.* He punched in Vince's cell phone number. No answer. He left a voice mail and moved to the check-in counter.

"Miss, could you tell me why flight 1920 has been delayed? I'm waiting for someone on that flight."

"Who are you waiting for, sir?"

"Mr. Vince Giardini."

"A relative?"

"My business partner. He boarded the plane at LAX, but called me when he was delayed in Albuquerque."

"Are you sure he continued on from Albuquerque?"

"He would have told me when he called if he was not

continuing onto Denver."

"Please leave your name and telephone number and we'll notify you just as soon as we know the status of the flight."

Sal's stomach knotted. He didn't feel good about the situation, and wondered if the plane had gone down. He went to the bar and ordered a beer. Another hour and a half went by. He telephoned Thomas.

"Vince's plane hasn't arrived. It took off from Albuquerque, but it's been delayed until further notice."

"It's probably due to bad weather. Keep me posted."

"I will."

Disconnecting, Sal ordered another drink. Before he finished it, his cell phone rang.

"Is this Mr. Catalano?"

"Yes"

"Mr. Catalano, officially we're not allowed to give this information out to anyone, except for relatives of the passenger. I understand that you're his partner and that the passenger doesn't have any close relatives except for his wife."

"That's right."

"I'm sorry to inform you that Mr. Giardini's flight is missing. He's on the manifest and checked in at LAX. He also re-boarded the plane in Albuquerque."

"How can you lose a plane?"

"The flight vanished from the screen. We haven't been able to contact the pilot. When we hear further, we will notify you or Mr. Giardini's wife."

"As I mentioned before, I would appreciate it if you would notify me first. I would prefer to notify Mrs. Giardini before the airlines do if it is bad news."

"I understand."

Sal rubbed his forehead. A headache was coming on, and

he hoped it was not going to be a vicious migraine. He pulled out his cell phone and called a nearby chain hotel. After he'd booked a reservation he waited for the hotel limo, feeling more and more uneasy as time went by. Once he'd checked in, he called the airline and left the hotel's number along with his room extension. Sleeping was all but impossible. He turned on the TV and watched the late night show. The cell phone rang. He hoped it was Vince telling him he'd arrived.

"Mr. Catalano?"

"Yes. Have you news of the flight?"

"Yes. We need to speak with Mrs. Giardini. We can't reach her with the number we have on record. Do you have another contact number?"

"No." His palms were damp. "What happened?"

"The plane crashed in the Rockies. There's not much left of it. As far as we know, there were no survivors. The only survivors of flight 1920 originating in LAX were those who departed the plane at Albuquerque and did not re-board."

"How many chose to cancel the flight when they deplaned at Albuquerque?"

"Four passengers departed the flight and requested that their luggage be taken off the plane."

"What about the passengers who carried their luggage onboard?"

The airline official sighed. "If they left the flight in Albuquerque they were handed a boarding card, which they would have had to give the agent when they re-boarded. Mr. Giardini handed in his boarding card."

"Is there any chance a passenger might have given his card to the agent when he re-boarded, then realized he'd left something behind and walked off the plane?"

"If our agent was busy or distracted, a passenger could

possibly have left the flight and not re-boarded."

Sal nodded. "What happened to the plane when it went down?"

"Evidently, there was a massive explosion upon impact. We have not, perhaps never will find the black boxes."

"Are you saying that there were no survivors?" Sal asked in a low tone.

"That's what I'm saying."

"Oh man." He hung up, called Thomas, and relayed what he had just been told.

"You need to call Danni before the airlines do. Personally, I don't think that Vince was on the plane. He's smarter than to board a plane that needs repairs. Let me know if you hear anything else. I don't feel much like skiing now, so I'll call Evelyn tonight, pass the news onto her, and go on back to Vegas tomorrow."

Chapter 4
A Storm Brews

Eddie pulled into the parking lot down the street from Danni's home at daybreak. As the sun rose over the Atlantic, casting its crimson and gold reflections upon the sea, Eddie took his bait bucket and fishing rod from the back of his vehicle and carried them up the beach to a spot near Danni's home. A half hour later, Danni jogged by him. Eddie turned and watched as she made her way down the beach. For the next hour, until she passed him again, Eddie appeared only to be an early morning fisherman, nothing more. A few joggers stopped and chatted, eyeing the few fish that he'd reeled in. Once he saw Danni return to her home and disappear from sight, Eddie gathered up his things and returned to his truck.

***

When Danni came in from her run on the beach, she poured herself a glass of cranberry juice and placed a bagel into the toaster. When it popped up, she placed it on a china plate, buttered it, and then layered it with a thin coating of light cream cheese. Placing her breakfast on a tray along with a napkin, she carried it out to the patio off the master bedroom, which faced the sea. She set the tray with her meager breakfast down on a small round glass table, and sat down in a white wicker loveseat to enjoy the view.

The sun was obscured by puffy light grey clouds that would soon evaporate, giving way to a beautiful sunny morning in Florida. She took a sip of cranberry juice, then set the glass back down, leaned back in the love seat, and closed her eyes for a moment. The sound of the surf soothed her as the tide rushed in. Seagulls cried to one another, while others sang their mysterious songs of the sea.

This special place, in Highlands Beach, between Boca Raton and Del Rey Beach, had been their home for nearly twenty years. The only thing that she and Vince had ever lacked in their life together was children, which they had both wanted. However, it was not to be. Not because of Vince, but because of her. She'd been to many doctors and specialists, but they had all agreed that nothing could be done about her condition. Finally, both she and Vince had accepted the fact. In the long run, it was best that they had not had children.

When Vince's partner had been killed, destiny had stepped in and they had adopted his son Bobby, who had since grown into a responsible and trustworthy adult and was currently in training at JVS to assume a position as a partner of the company.

Until five years ago, she and Vince had been happy together, living, traveling, and working together. However, since then, their romance had cooled. Sex had become almost non-existent in their relationship. Knowing Vince as intimately as she did, she began to suspect that either there was something physically wrong with him or he was having an affair. The strong scent of floral perfume that so often clung to his suit jackets, as well as the pink lipstick smears that stained the collars of his shirts when she washed them, more or less confirmed her suspicions that something was wrong in their marriage. It also lent support to her premise of him having an affair. Despite the physical evidence that confronted her, she remained adamant in her belief that happily married men do not have affairs. Perhaps they only need to talk things out.

When she finished her light breakfast, she rose, carried the tray back into the kitchen, and set it on the counter. She then moved into her bedroom, stripped out of her jogging clothes, showered, toweled off, perfumed, and dressed. After applying the finishing touches to her makeup, she slipped into her dress and stepped into a pair of stiletto heels. She took her oversized leather handbag, hitched it over her shoulder, and dashed out to where Vince's brand new red Ferrari was parked.

***

When Eddie, who had been vigilantly watching the house, heard the Ferrari's engine start, he glanced over and saw Danni pull out of her driveway and head north on AIA. He started his engine and followed her, careful to maintain what he felt was an appropriate distance behind her to avoid being seen.

***

Danni glanced at her watch. She was running late. She shrugged her shoulders. There was nothing she could do about it. Lainey would just have to wait for her and find some way to entertain herself. Danni knew the shops on Worth Avenue had already opened, and she figured Lainey would take a stroll, browsing through the shops and the galleries while she waited.

As she continued her drive up the coastal route on A1A from Highlands Beach, she turned on the radio and caught the end of a newscast, which briefly mentioned an airline crash in the Rockies. She drew her fine brows together. Vince was to have met Sal and Thomas in Denver. She reached over and fished in her handbag for her cell phone. When she discovered it wasn't there, she reflected for a moment and then remembered. It was still at home charging.

Realizing there was nothing more she could do at the moment, she continued and exited A1A when she reached Lantana.

***

Eddie stayed with her the entire drive, but when she made the turn off A1A, he dropped back another car's length to avoid getting too close to the Ferrari. When her turn signal flashed on near the coffee shop, he pulled over, parked near a news stand, stepped out of his pick up, and bought the last paper. As he was opening the paper, he happened to glance to his watch and knew it was time to go back to Pompano, clean up, and drive over to see Tiffany.

***

After Danni had pulled into a parking space near a coffee house, she turned off the engine, dashed in, and ordered a cappuccino with a double shot of espresso. Setting the drink down on the nearest table, she spotted pages of the Palm Beach Post scattered on the table next to hers. Today's copy, it contained only the sports page and the life style sections. The front page was missing. Taking the life style section, she sat down and read it from cover to cover while she enjoyed her drink. When she'd finished the cappuccino, she rose and moved to the newspaper stand to purchase a fresh copy of today's paper. There was not a copy left. Disappointed, she left.

When she finally arrived Palm Beach, she went directly to the restaurant where she was to meet Lainey. She wasn't there. The maître d', noticing her disappointment, came over to inquire as to the cause of her concern and how he might be of assistance. When Danni explained her dilemma, he told her that Lainey had called and left a message for her, stating that she wouldn't be able to make it today. Disappointed, Danni had lunch alone. Afterward, she went to the Galleria del Sol. The painting she'd admired the last time she had visited was not to be found in the gallery. When she inquired about it, the clerk told her that the

15

owner of the gallery had taken the painting home.

"Oh!" she said with a sigh. "I had my heart set on it."

"If you will excuse me for a moment, I'll make a phone call. It may still be for sale." The clerk moved into the other room and returned a few seconds later.

"Are you Mrs. Giardini?"

"Yes, I am."

"The owner said to tell you, it's yours. You may pick it up next week."

"Not today?"

"No, I'm sorry."

"I suppose I could come back. I really love that painting."

"Wonderful. We'll look forward to seeing you next week."

"All right." She exhaled a dissatisfied sigh and glanced at her watch. Almost three p.m. *Why am I rushing? It's not like I have to be any special place at any specific time.*

On previous visits, she'd always wanted to stay at the historical Grand Duchess Hotel, which was located on Worth Avenue, just a few blocks away from the gallery but still close to the beach. The hotel had been built in 1926, and with its many well-known guests had become famous over the years. So she decided that now would be the time to do something she'd always wanted to.

When she arrived at the three-story hotel built in a Spanish-Moorish style, she strolled through an intimate courtyard, lush with palms and a fountain. She paused just long enough to admire her surroundings. Ambling into the reception area, the corners of her lips tilted up. The lobby was charming, and reminded her of an English country home; one that she and Vince had once vacationed in.

She walked over to the registration desk and said, "Good afternoon. I'm Mrs. Vince Giardini. I realize it's the middle of the season, but I'm hoping that you have either a non-smoking single room or a small suite available."

"I'm happy to say that I have just had a cancellation. We have a beautiful one-bedroom mini-suite available. Would that be acceptable?"

"That would be perfect."

"It's so nice to see you back again. How is Mr. Giardini? He's not ill, is he? This is the first time that I remember seeing you alone."

Taken aback by his statement, she was silent a moment. Knowing she and Vince had never stayed at this hotel, she drew her brows together and asked, "Do you know Vince, my husband?"

"Why yes, of course. I must say that you're looking quite well, Mrs. Giardini. You've lost weight, haven't you? And your hair is a little different; longer than usual, I think. It's a very attractive look on you."

"Thank you, but you must be thinking of another Giardini. I've never been here before," she replied, trying to maintain her composure.

The clerk paled. "I'm sorry. I must have been mistaken. We, ah…have several Giardini's that stay here regularly. Since you haven't stayed with us before, I'll have the bellman show you around. I believe you will find The Grand Duchess to be everything you could possibly want."

She smiled. "I'm sure I will. Thank you so much."

From the little she'd seen, the hotel promised to be everything she'd heard it was and more. When she walked into the library, she paused at the entry. Wood paneled, with a fireplace, and English hunting prints on the wall, the room offered overstuffed seating, books, newspapers, DVD's, and a flat-screen computer. A man sat in front of it. He turned, almost as though he knew he were being observed, and glanced her way. When his gaze fell upon her, his eyes brightened, and he smiled. From where she stood, she could see he had a deep tan, curly, sandy-blond hair, and a dark mustache. He was incredibly handsome. The edges of her lips tilted up.

"I hope I'm not disturbing you."

"Not at all, At least, not my work." His voice was low and clear.

"You may use this room anytime you like, madam." The bellman's deep voice interrupted the mood at that moment, and abruptly jarred her back into reality. "We also have a fabulous restaurant and lounge."

She nodded. At the moment, she wasn't interested in the restaurant or the lounge. She wanted to stay in the library with this compelling man. She knew she'd met him before, at Lainey's party. She was nearly certain it was him, but she didn't remember his name. She brought her attention back to the present, turned to the bellman, and said, "I'll be having dinner here tonight."

"Excellent decision, madam. The cuisine is marvelous. We also have music and dancing after nine p.m. You will enjoy it. With your permission, I'll make the reservation for you. Would eight-thirty be convenient?"

She nodded. "I'll look forward to it."

"If you're ready, I'll take your packages to your room."

"If you would, please. Thank you."

***

Once the bellman had left her room, she kicked off her red stiletto heels and stripped down to a lacy red bra and thongs. She sat down on the bed and made a telephone call to Vince on the hotel phone. No answer. She left a message. Then she called Lainey. No answer. She clicked off, deciding not to leave a message but to call again later. Since she was staying over, maybe she could convince Lainey to come up tomorrow and they could spend some time together. If not, she would stop by and visit her in Vero on her way back home.

Lying down on the bed to relax a moment, she drew a blanket over herself, closed her eyes, and fell fast asleep, not awakening until nearly seven-thirty p.m. Revived, she showered, dressed, and left the room. On her way to the restaurant, she stopped to admire each of the paintings on the walls.

Strolling through the hotel, she rounded a corner and bumped into a gentleman coming her way. "Oh! I'm sorry for being so clumsy." Danni's face heated as she saw that it was the same man she'd seen in the library.

Noticing her discomfort, he smiled and then laughed. "This must be fate. I'd been hoping to see you again. Unfortunately, I'm on my way out. I'm Peter Langley, and I'm sorry to say, because I know we've met before, your name has slipped my mind."

"Danni Giardini."

"I wish I could stay and invite you to have a cocktail with me, but I'm in a bit of a rush. Perhaps we'll meet again soon."

CHAPTER 5
CONFIRMATION

Sal stood waiting in the baggage claim area of the Palm Beach Airport for his luggage to arrive from Denver. He was in no rush. He dreaded the task that lay ahead of him. The last thing that he wanted to do was to inform his best friend's wife, the woman he'd known and loved that her husband had been killed or was missing. He prayed that she hadn't read the headlines this morning, and hoped that the airline officials had not reached her by telephone.

But when he glanced at the front page of The Palm Beach Post that he'd just picked up in a gift shop he'd passed on his way to baggage claim, his worst fear slapped him right in the face. Damn! Based on what he was presently looking at, it was more than likely that Danni had seen the article. Now he was even more concerned that he hadn't been able to reach her by telephone or in person, having been delayed leaving Denver by the winter storm that had moved in.

Later, once he'd unpacked his luggage and settled in at home, he realized he couldn't delay the inevitable any longer. He would try contacting Danni one more time, and if that was unsuccessful, he would have to go over to hers and Vince's home to tell her personally. But before he could punch in the numbers, his own phone rang.

"Hello?"

"Is this Sal Catalano, Mr. Giardini's partner?"

"Yes. Who is this?"

"This is Mr. Barrows. I represent the airline that Mr. Giardini was traveling on from Los Angeles to Denver. I'm afraid the news concerning Mr. Giardini still isn't very good."

Sal groaned. "I know. I've already read the headlines in the local newspaper."

"I'm terribly sorry about that. They weren't supposed to print anything yet, not until all of the passengers' relatives had been notified. I'm not surprised though. This happens more often than it should."

"I've noticed."

"In any case, since you are our only family contact, I can tell you that, according to our records, your partner checked one piece of luggage onboard flight 1920. Our records show that it wasn't taken off the plane, nor was it transferred to another aircraft in Albuquerque. We believe Mr. Giardini was aboard the flight when it crashed. The agent at the gate took a boarding pass from him when the passengers reboarded the plane on its leg from Albuquerque to Denver. We still haven't been able to reach Mrs. Giardini. We'll continue down the list and come back to her later.

"Thank you for keeping me up to date." Despite what he'd just been told, Sal refused to give up hope, and thought to himself, *Oh man! If you're still alive, Vince, and I pray you are, I hope to God you call me soon.*

Chapter 6
Suspicion

The moment Danni opened the front door, she heard the phone ringing. She raced to answer it.

"Hello? Oh, Sal. I've tried so many times in the last day or so to reach Vince. I thought this must be him calling. Is anything wrong?"

"I'm not sure yet."

"What do you mean you're not sure?"

Figuring there was no way he could put this off, he said, "The plane that Vince boarded at LAX had some problems and made an emergency landing in Albuquerque, where they intended to make repairs."

"And?" She sat down, concerned about what news was coming next.

"They didn't have the parts in Albuquerque, nor was there another aircraft to use for the flight from Albuquerque on into Denver. The captain deemed the plane safe to fly on into Denver; however, the passengers were given the option to continue onto Denver on that flight or to seek others."

Feeling a ray of hope, she asked, "So then, is Vince still in Albuquerque trying to find another flight into Denver?"

"I don't know. We don't know what he did. None of us have

22

heard from him since the last time he called to tell me the plane had stopped in Albuquerque for repairs."

"So where is flight #1920 now?"

Sal cleared his throat and paused before answering. "According to what I've been told, it crashed in the Rockies last night."

"Oh, my God!" Danni's voice rose to a high pitch. "Are you telling me that the flight that Vince was on has crashed?"

"We don't know that yet. He may have gotten off the plane in Albuquerque and never reboarded."

"What about his checked luggage?"

"To the best of anyone's knowledge, it was still on the aircraft."

"Oh no!" Now standing, she grabbed onto the edge of the counter to steady herself. "But that doesn't necessarily mean he was." She knew she was grasping at proverbial straws, but right now, that was all she had.

"No. It doesn't. The airlines should be calling you soon with another update. But remember, no matter what they tell you, until there is physical evidence available to support his having been killed in the crash of Flight 1920, no one knows where Vince is. He's always been a survivor. I'm back home now, so if you don't have plans for dinner tonight, I'd like to pick you up for an early dinner, let's say about five, in Del Rey at Bella's, where we can talk more about this."

"I'm really not very hungry, but I don't want to stay here alone tonight either. If I do, I'll end up pacing the floor all evening and be up all night waiting to hear from Vince. Maybe he was on the flight and I never will hear from him again, but it seems to me that he would have stayed overnight in Albuquerque and caught the first plane out to Denver in the morning, rather than boarding a plane that required repairs."

Sal sighed. "Honestly Danni, I wish I knew what he actually did do. But, I sure hope you're right. Thomas doesn't believe he was on the plane either. I'll see you soon. Bring your cell phone. We'll keep both of our phones on just in case he calls."

***

Just as she was stepping into her stilettos, the home phone rang again. She hurried into the next room to pick it up, but stumbled on her way. Fortunately, she caught her fall and was able to steady her just as she passed the sofa. By the time she reached the phone, the caller had hung up. Had it been Vince? But, when she checked the caller ID, the number on the last call had been an 800 number.

To add to the chaos of the moment, the doorbell rang. Assuming it must be Sal, she called out, "Come in" and moved to open the front door.

"Danni, how are you?" Sal asked, his dark brown eyes reflecting his concern. .

"Okay for the moment," she replied. "It's so comforting to see you. Have you heard any further from the airlines?"

"Nothing concrete. Right now, you know everything that I do."

"Odd. I just received a call from an 800 number. When I picked the phone up, whoever was on the other end of the line had hung up. Do you think that might have been the airlines?"

"Maybe. We'll talk about it at dinner. If you're ready, we need to be going. Are you hungry?"

"No, but I missed lunch and I need to eat something to keep my strength up."

"Then, let's go."

***

Right after they had been seated at the restaurant, they began to talk. Danni's eyes misted over as they spoke about Vince, and the strong possibility that he'd been on the plane that had crashed.

Sal heaved a sigh and offered, "We may never know what happened to the passengers. They haven't found anything, not even the black boxs."

I think that we must face the facts. Neither of us has heard from Vince since the last time you spoke to him. He'd have called if he'd aborted the flight at Albuquerque, if for no other reason than to advise you of his new arrival time. Vince evidently was one of the passengers that died when the plane exploded, unless...."

"Unless?"

"Unless he left the plane in Albuquerque and took the opportunity to begin a new life."

"But he had no reason on Earth to want to begin over again."

"He might have." A hint of sorrow filled her lovely voice.

Bemused, Sal asked, "Why? In spite of the economy, JVS is a successful business. Vince had plenty of money...everything he ever wanted too, include a happy marriage with a wonderful woman. You and Vince were happy, weren't you?"

Her left eyebrow arched.

"Would you like to tell me about it?" Sal asked in a subdued low voice.

Danni hesitated before replying. "The past five years have not been so happy. In fact, I have reason to believe that Vince had a mistress. What if he wanted to be with her? Though I'm a convert to the Catholic religion, Vince has been Catholic all of his life. As you know, Catholics aren't allowed to divorce and then remarry."

Sal shook his head. "As long as I've known Vince, he's adored you. What's led you to believe that he may have had another woman?"

"It's a long story."

"I have all the time in the world tonight. But, let's order first." Sal motioned to the waiter then turned back to Danni. "Do you know what you would like?"

"An antipasto salad with a side of spaghetti, and a glass of merlot would be nice."

"Are you sure you don't want to order a full entrée?"

"Not tonight."

Sal ordered the same for himself, realizing that he wasn't so hungry either. When the waiter finally moved away from the table, Sal leaned back in his chair and said, "Okay. I'm waiting to hear about you and Vince, and your relationship of late."

She took a deep breath, exhaled, and began. "The last time I was in Palm Beach, I stayed overnight at a boutique hotel, The Grand Duchess. I'd never stayed there before, and didn't think that Vince had either. The desk clerk insisted that he knew Vince, and that he'd met me numerous times. He mentioned that I had changed my hairstyle and lost weight since he'd last seen me."

"He was obviously mistaken. Maybe he was new."

"That's what I thought at first, but I discovered that he'd been employed there for some time."

"That's odd." Sal drew his thick black brows together. "Did anything else happen?"

"No. Except that the waiter thought that he'd met me as well."

"Huh."

"It would appear that Vince has stayed there more than once, with a woman who he introduced as his wife."

"Maybe there's another explanation," Sal said, reaching for straws.

"Like what? I don't think so." Danni shook her head. "Besides, there's more."

"More?"

"I found a tube of pink lipstick in his car. Oh, perhaps you could say a client had dropped her lipstick in his car, but he's come home with his shirts stained with the same shade of lipstick, and the heavy scent of a floral perfume clinging to his jackets."

"Hmm. You don't wear floral scents, nor have I ever seen you in pink."

"Exactly."

"When he returns, I'll have a talk with him."

"If he returns. And if he doesn't, I don't suppose we'll ever know."

"Probably not."

"Honestly, and this is going to sound selfish, but it would be easier for me to accept his death if it turns out he'd actually had a mistress. Of course, I'd be furious and sad at the same time," Danni continued.

"Much as I hate to admit it, for the first time in my life, I don't envy him."

***

Just then Sal's cell phone rang, creating a welcome interruption in the intensity to the moment.

"Hello?"

"Mr. Catalano?"

"Yes, this is he."

"Sir. this is Mr. Barrows with the airlines again. I'm calling to let you know we haven't been able to reach Mrs. Giardini."

"She's with me now."

"Then, I need to speak with her."

"Have you found anything new?" Sal asked. "I'd like to be ready to help her if there is bad news."

"Well, Mr. Catalano, we found a watch among the wreckage. It was damaged and charred, but we were able to discern the initials VG engraved on the back. We believe that the watch

27

may have been Mr. Giardini's. As such, we're presuming that he perished in the explosion following the crash."

Sal shook his head in denial. "Thank you for telling me first."

"Now, may I please speak with Mrs. Giardini?"

"Of course." Sal handed the phone to Danni. "It's the airline, and it's not good news."

Danni took the phone and listened without speaking. Shocked from what she was hearing, she blanched. When Mr. Barrows was finished, she thanked him, clicked off the phone, and handed it back to Sal.

"Vince wore that watch religiously. The only time he ever took it off was when he was taking a shower or involved with water sports."

"We need to call Bobby."

"I don't know if we can reach him, but we can try."

"Why wouldn't we be able to contact him?"

"He's in Mexico right now, on a surf trip." Danni took another sip of wine. "I'll call him in the morning."

***

When Danni awoke the next morning, her first thought was of Vince. She felt a heaviness in her heart and a deep sadness. She'd married him for all the right reasons. Whether or not he'd died in the crash or had lost his heart to another woman, she'd lost someone she dearly loved. She struggled to drag herself out of bed. With a slight headache from the wine that she'd drunk last night, she dressed in her jogging clothes.

A chill was in the air when she stepped out of the house. There weren't many people out at this hour; only a lone fisherman down the beach. She decided she wasn't up to jogging, turned, and went back into the house. Once inside, she poured a cup of coffee, then went into the living room, turned on the television, and settled into her favorite chair to watch the news. They were focusing on the crash and the fact that, according to the reports, no one could have possibly survived it.

The house phone rang. Danni rose to answer. It was Bobby.

"I just saw the news. Uncle Vince was on that plane, wasn't he?"

"Yes. I'm sorry I didn't have a chance to tell you before you heard it on the news."

"I'm really gonna' miss him."

"We all will."

"Are you okay, Aunt Danni?"

"Yes, honey. I'm okay."

"He's all right, Danni. He was a good man. He's in a good place. Don't worry about him. Life doesn't end at death. I think it's like walking through a door. There's no pause between life and death. It's not like everything goes black and you're scared, suffocating; don't know what to do or where to go."

"I don't think dying is anything to be afraid of," Danni said, attempting to reassure him.

"But everyone is."

"Because, whatever faith we are of, we are uncertain of what we will discover, if anything, after we die."

"I've been going to church down here, and have developed a strong faith in God. Besides that, surfing is kind of a spiritual experience. Are you sure you're okay?"

"I'm okay. It's just hard to believe that Vince is never coming home again." *Of course, it would have been the same if he'd left me for another woman. And maybe he did.* She sighed. "Dying is something that we all must do. No man ever has escaped death. From the moment we are born, our destination draws closer."

"Yeah. And no one knows when death will come. The best thing to do is just do your best and help others along their way."

"Well said. When are you coming home?"

"If you're sure you're all right, I'd like to stay for a few more days, but I definitely want to be there for Uncle Vince's memorial service."

"Sal and I need to make arrangements. I'll let you know when it will be held. Will we be able to reach you on your cell?"

"Maybe not. I'm out of range most of the time. I'll call you next week at this same time. Tell Sal I'll be ready to get back to work. I won't stay down here much longer. I know that with being two hands short, Sal is overloaded. Don't be surprised if he puts you to work in the office."

"It might be good for me. I can handle most anything he assigns to me unless it involves numbers."

Bobby laughed. "That's partially my job. Keep your chin up, Aunt Danni. We're all going to miss Uncle Vince, but Sal and I will be there for you."

"I know you will," Danni said, beginning to choke up.

"I love you."

"I love you, too. Be careful down there."

CHAPTER 7
FATE INTERVENES

Two cities south of Boca Raton, in Pompano Beach, Eddie Haywood popped open a cold bottle of beer. He grabbed the newspaper from the end table, sat down on the sofa, and kicked back, propping his feet up on the coffee table.

Flight #1920 had crashed into the mountains near Denver. All passengers, including the crew, were killed upon impact. Vince Giardini, President of JVS Development, was listed as one of the passengers onboard. A memorial service would be held at St. Lucy's Catholic Church in Highlands Beach on Sunday at 4:00 PM.

Photos were shown of Vince and his lovely widow, Danni.

Eddie sat up and set his beer on the coffee table. Man! There she was, a grieving widow, and in his mind, a perfect target for opportunity! He hadn't had to lift a finger. Fate had been on his side. God! What a good lookin' woman, all dressed up. He whistled. *She's going to need help now; especially with her lawn. Bet her gardener quits.* He laughed. *She'll need a handyman, too. That's me. I can sure use the money right now. Hell, I think I'll drive up tomorrow morning and inquire. If there's a position open as her employee, I won't need to fish behind her house anymore to keep an eye on her, or to catch a glance at her firm derriere as she jogs past me on the beach.*

Out of curiosity, he turned to the classifieds. Scanning them, he found there was an ad for a gardener in Highlands Beach. Could he get so lucky? Hell yes, he could. Over the years, he'd seen his luck go from bad to good. When it was bad, no one could be more down. When it was good, it was spectacular. He moved to the phone and punched in the number from the ad.

Three hours later, Eddie arrived at Danni's home for his interview. The following day, he reported for work. The lawn would be perfect for the memorial party.

CHAPTER 8
DEVINE APPOINTMENTS

On the day of the service, the cold front that had been predicted moved in. The entire United States dipped down into freezing temperatures. Florida hadn't had weather this cold since the late fifties. People who normally wore lightweight clothing rushed out to purchase sweaters, sweats, and coats. Surprisingly, everyone from out of state arrived just in time for the service, in spite of the cold weather and travel delays in Chicago, Denver, Baltimore, and New York.

Clients, distant friends, and acquaintances crammed into the church. Some stood, crowded into the back. Eddie stood in the crowd near the doorway. An employee of Mrs. Giardini's now, it wouldn't make any difference if he was seen or not. After the celebration of Vince's life, all of their close friends and family gathered, not on the beach as had been planned, but in Danni's warm home for a memorial party.

Their closest friends, Thomas and Evelyn, stayed on for another week, and together with her sister, Lainey, and Dr. Sam's wife, Vivian, they cleared Vince's personal belongings from Danni's luxurious home on the beach. Not wanting her to go through the stressful ordeal of removing Vince's personal possessions, they sent her off to Palm Beach to relax, visit a spa, and enjoy herself as much as she could under the circumstances.

***

Driving north up A1A to Palm Beach, Danni took a deep breath, and promised herself she would enjoy her time away in spite of the tragedy surrounding Vince's death; or if he hadn't died in the crash, she would stop thinking about his departure from her life. It was a beautiful day, and temperatures had returned to the mid-seventies, which was normal for mid-January in Florida. The Atlantic was a brilliant royal blue, with white caps rolling onto shore. White cumulous clouds built in the distance. After checking into the Grand Duchess Hotel, she arranged a massage and a facial for the afternoon.

When she left the spa, she came straight back to her room reeking of the strong scent of lavender from the oil that the massage therapist had used. Stripping all of her clothes off and leaving them in a pile on the floor, she headed toward the shower, washed her hair, and banished the unwanted scent from her body. Stepping out of the steaming shower, she toweled herself dry, smoothed lotion on her body from head to toe, and sprayed on her favorite perfume on. Finally, after styling and blow drying her hair, she touched it up with a flat iron and dressed for a stroll down Worth Avenue.

By evening she had an armful of packages, which contained small gifts for all of her friends who had helped her through this trying time in her life. Entering through the arch of the patio of the hotel, she literally bumped into a tall gentleman on his way out. Stepping back, she glanced up to see that it was the same compelling stranger she'd seen on her earlier trip to Palm Beach.

"Oh! I'm so sorry." She stooped to retrieve her handbag that she'd dropped.

"Please, allow me. It was my fault. I wasn't looking where I was going. I had my mind on something else." He bent and retrieved her bag and gathered up the items that had fallen out, and were now scattered all over the Saltillo walkway.

As he stood up, the corners of his mouth turned up in an amused smile as his warm sparkling eyes of amber met hers. She warmed as his gaze held hers. Uncomfortably aware that she was blushing, she took the purse that he was now offering her and thanked him.

"You're more than welcome. Didn't I run into you here a few weeks ago?"

"You were the gentlemen in the library working on the computer, weren't you?"

He nodded. "And I was also the person that you literally ran into in the lounge, Peter Langley. Call me Pete, please," he said extending his hand to shake hers.

"Danni Giardini," she said, shaking his hand. She smiled, more than pleased to meet him. His hand was warm, his handshake strong. "I believe we've met before. I mean, other than in the library and in the lounge."

"I'm not great with names, but I always remember faces, especially beautiful ones. When I saw you a few weeks ago, you looked familiar. I believe I met you for the first time a few months ago, at a party in Vero Beach."

"That's right," she said. "It was at Lainey, my sister's, home. It was the last time that she was in town with her husband."

He smiled, his amber eyes twinkling. "It's great to see you again."

"And you too. I'm afraid that I, er…wasn't really looking where I was going."

He chuckled. "Don't worry about it. You did say your last name was Giardini, didn't you?"

"Yes."

"You're not related to Vince Giardini by any chance, are

you?"

"Er…I'm his—"

"His much younger sister, perhaps? Then you must know Madison. She and Vince are great friends."

"Madison? No. I've never met her." Danni wore a puzzled expression upon her face. "Is she your wife?"

Pete chuckled. "No. I'm not married. She's my cousin."

She smiled as she thought about what she'd just learned. *He's not married. I wonder how Vince knew his cousin.*

***

"She owns Madison's Books just up the road, north of Juno Beach. In fact, you resemble each other."

"Really?"

He nodded. "She's a beautiful woman, a little taller than you, shorter hair, and not quite as slender. Do you live here, on this coast?"

"We live…er…I live in Highlands Beach. I haven't been to north of Palm Beach in years, except to visit friends in Vero."

"You're not married, are you?" Could this be Vince's wife? Not only he, but also Madison, had been under the distinct impression that Vince was single.

A shadow crossed her face. "I was married. Ah…Vince, my husband, was killed in a plane crash a couple of weeks ago. I'm his widow."

"I am so sorry." *My God! Madison doesn't know.* "That wasn't the crash in the Rockies that killed everyone on board, was it?"

"Yes."

"That was a tragic accident…not only tragic, but gruesome as well. I am so sorry to hear of your loss."

***

"Thank you for your kind words. It was terrible. Since I've learned of the tragedy, my friends have been so kind to me. In fact, they sent me to Palm Beach this weekend while they clear my home of my husband's personal items." A tear trickled down her cheek. She brushed it away. "I'm sorry. I still can't believe that Vince is dead. He was my best friend except that...." *It's looking as though he betrayed me.* She'd almost said that. Why? Whether she was attracted to Pete or not, whether or not she had met him before, he was still a virtual stranger to her.

He took a handkerchief from his pocket and offered it to her.

"Thank you. I didn't know people still carried hankies."

"I'm an exception, I guess. Look, I haven't had dinner yet, have you?"

She shook her head. The corners of her mouth turned up as she gazed into his sparkling amber eyes. "No."

"Okay, then, I'd like to visit with you more. Would you join me around seven-thirty in the lounge? We can have a drink, and then move into the dining room. They have wonderful food here."

"Thank you. I'd enjoy the company."

"That's settled then. I'll see you in the lounge at seven-thirty."

Danni's heart lightened. She walked into the lobby, checked in, and went to her fabulous room. Once inside, she set her packages down and turned on soft classical music on the radio. After relaxing for a short time, she dressed for the evening in what she felt was one of her most becoming dresses. She left the room and strolled into the lounge, where she was met at the door by a host who escorted her to a corner booth where Pete was waiting.

"You look beautiful tonight," Pest said as he rose to greet her.

"Thank you."

"Would you like a glass of champagne?"

"Yes," Danni smiled. "I'd love a glass of champagne."

After they had ordered drinks and appetizers, Pete asked,

"What, if you don't mind my asking, other than your friends sending you off, brings you to Palm Beach again so soon?"

"No. I don't mind. Besides shopping and relaxation, I'm going to pick up a painting that I purchased a couple of weeks ago."

The corners of his mouth turned up, and with that, she noticed for the first time that he had dimples. Her attraction toward him accelerated. He was one of the most handsome men she'd ever met, to include most of the well-known actors, one of which was considered to be the sexiest man alive. Vince had been nice looking, but more in a rugged sort of way.

"I paint a little myself. It's a hobby, but I often dream of it someday being my vocation. In fact, I have a couple of oil paintings on consignment in a gallery nearby. I'm curious, what gallery are you dealing with?"

"The Galleria Del Sol."

"It is a small world. That's where my paintings are hanging."

"I'd love to see them. Are they seascapes or…?"

"One is a seascape; the other is of a child playing on the beach. When are you going to pick up your painting?"

"I thought I'd do that just before I leave on Monday."

"Good. Look, if it wouldn't be an inconvenience, I'd like to meet you there at the gallery. I'll show you my work then. Would you like to do that?" He withdrew a card from his pocket and handed it to her.

"That would be wonderful." She glanced down at his card. "Your card reads Peter L. Stevens, not Langley. Do artists have pseudonyms?"

He smiled as his eyes met hers. "In this case, yes. My biological father's name was Stevens. He was killed when I was a child. In real life, er…my career, I go by my stepfather's name of Langley."

"And in real life you are...."

"A financial consultant."

***

"You must have met Vince through business," she commented, slipping his card into her bag.

He was going to need to take that and run with it. He wasn't much of a financial consultant in that he didn't have an office, but he did have a knack for choosing the right stocks, and had assisted many divorcees and widows. He hadn't helped Vince financially either, but telling this gorgeous woman that he had was far more preferable than the truth. Vince had been staying with Madison for a weekend. He'd been there most of the time working on a painting of the intra-coastal, but they'd all gotten together for a barbecue that Saturday night.

Putting the relationship between his cousin and Vince aside for a moment, Pete considered it destiny that he'd literally run into Danni again. He'd been afraid he'd never see her again, that it had been a lifetime coincidence when he'd seen her in the library. He'd chastised himself later that he hadn't remembered her name from the party, nor had he asked for her card. Vince had been a fool to jeopardize his relationship with her.

CHAPTER 9
THE ACCIDENT

Danni checked out of the hotel and headed toward the gallery just in time to meet Pete. Nearly there, she pulled into a parking spot just up the street from the gallery. Butterflies danced in her stomach in her excitement to see Pete. When she stepped into the gallery, she was crestfallen that he wasn't there. Maybe he'd forgotten.

***

Pete watched from across the street as Danni came out of the gallery. With a slight frown on her lovely face, she walked down the street to her parking place. Sliding into the bright red new Ferrari, she pulled out, not seeing the car that was racing down the street. There was no way the driver had time to brake. Pete flinched as it struck her left front fender. Aghast, he saw it speed off. He was so shocked that he failed to get the license plate. All he could recall was that it was a pea green older model van, which didn't look as if it belonged in the area. Damn! Danni could have been hurt.

She turned to look behind her to see what happened and noticed the van speeding away. "Damn!" she yelled, smacking the leather steering wheel with the side of her fist. She pulled back into the parking place, parked, and jumped out of the car.

Throwing her arms out to her sides, hands palms up, she yelled, "Hey! Come back here!" Her efforts were to no avail. Frustrated, she ran her fingers through her hair and stomped back into the gallery.

Pete exhaled a deep breath. Whew! If she was injured, she wasn't hurt badly. He could see that she was angry and had more than likely gone into the gallery to place a call to the police, and another to the insurance company. He crossed the street and headed toward the gallery, intending to help her deal with the officers and the insurance company.

"Pete! Am I glad to see you?"

"I'm sorry, I'm late. I know I was to meet you earlier, but I was detained by a client. I just saw what happened."

"Did you get the license plate number by any chance?" Danni asked.

"I'm sorry, I didn't. The van was speeding, and quite honestly, I was more concerned about you. I was afraid you had been hurt. I can't believe they didn't stop."

"Thank God I'm all in one piece, and you saw them hit me."

"It wasn't your fault. They should have slowed down."

"I should have seen it coming."

"Don't tell anyone else that," Pete advised.

"Would you stay here with me so that you can tell the police and my insurance agent what you saw?"

"I'll be glad to."

It was as Pete had said, and obvious to the police and to the insurance agent that the car that had struck Danni's had been speeding. There were several other witnesses who had seen the van strike the Ferrari and speed off. The insurance agent gave her an estimate and wrote her a check. "If you would like to have your car towed to the body shop now, I can provide you with a loaner."

"You might as well do that. I'll take you to the body shop," Pete offered.

"If you wouldn't mind."

"If I wouldn't mind? Of course not. I'll be more than happy to go with you."

"Thank you, Pete. Oh! I still don't have my painting."

"We can pick it up now. I'll set it in my trunk and we can transfer it to the loaner later."

"That would be great. I'm still looking forward to seeing your paintings."

"You will," Pete said with a wide grin. "We can meet back here at the gallery after you pick up your loaner. If you have time, we can have a glass of iced tea somewhere before you start back to Highlands Beach."

CHAPTER 10
FRIENDS

Evelyn glanced at her watch. "It's getting late. Danni should have been back by now."

"She'll be okay." Lainey said, attempting to reassure her. "She probably just got carried away shopping and lost track of time."

"I think I'll give her a call anyway."

"Wait. Someone just pulled into the driveway. It's probably Danni."

"That's not her car."

Lainey laughed. "No. It's definitely not a Ferrari."

"Let's go see who it is. If it's Danni, she may need help carrying packages."

***

Danni was just opening the trunk when Lainey and Evelyn appeared at her side. "Look at this! Not only do I have the painting I've been wanting for so long, but I purchased two more and I met the artist." Danni removed the paintings from the trunk with care.

Each of the women carried a painting in and set them against a wall in the living room.

"Oh! These are gorgeous! I especially like the child playing on the beach. It reminds me so much of my daughter, Chrissie, when she was that age."

"It does. Your daughter is so adorable, Evelyn. I wish you could have brought her with you."

"So do I, but I think Vince's memorial service would have disturbed her. We left her with Julie. They're having fun practicing their new routine for their upcoming show next February. I know that's a long time from now, but you should make plans and come to Vegas. Chrissie would be so excited."

"I'd love to."

"Plan on it. You can stay with us."

A loud knock sounded at the door, along with the sound of the doorbell.

Danni turned to walk back into the entry hall. "I'll get it. Sal!" she blurted out as she opened the door.

"Hey, beautiful!" He reached out and embraced her in a bear hug. "Glad you're back. On the way over, I stopped by Bella's and brought a couple of pizzas by for you girls. You haven't had dinner yet, have you?"

"No. Come on in. I just drove in from Palm Beach."

"You brought some beautiful paintings back," Sal said. "What happened to the Ferrari?"

"Someone hit me while I was pulling out of a parking place. It was a hit and run. They were speeding."

"You weren't hurt, were you?"

"Thankfully, no."

"Where's the car now?"

"At the body shop in Palm Beach being repaired. The insurance is paying for the loaner, and will deliver the Ferrari after it's fixed. Come and see my paintings. They're gorgeous, aren't they? I just couldn't resist. I was just going to buy the large seascape, but I fell in love with the others too. A man by the name of Peter L. Stevens painted the smaller ones. He knew Vince."

"How did he meet him?"

"Through his cousin, Madison Langley. She owns a bookstore just north of Juno Beach."

Sal's left eyebrow shot up. "Vince didn't read much. I wonder what he was doing in a bookstore. Is that where he met him?"

"I'm not sure. Career wise, Pete is a financial consultant."

"Where's his office?"

"I didn't ask. Palm Beach, I guess."

"Does he work for an investment company?"

"I don't think so. I think he's an independent financial consultant."

Sal drew his brows together. "The next time you see him, ask. Did he give you a card?"

"He did, but it relates to his paintings."

"Doesn't sound like he does much consulting."

Danni shrugged her shoulders. "Painting is Pete's hobby, but one he wishes to make his career."

"I know Pete," Lainey said. "In fact, he attended the party that I gave in Vero the last time that I was in town. Both Running Deer and I like him very much. We met him at the Galleria Del Sol while he was having a show."

"Well, that's interesting. Unfortunately, I was out of town and missed your party, but I'll look forward to meeting Mr. Langley in the future. He certainly seems to have cheered you up, Danni."

"Yes, he did."

"Running Deer will be here next week. I'd like both you and Sal to come and visit us while he's in town."

"I'd love to," Danni said.

***

"I'm sorry to change the subject," Sal said, "but did you girls already take Vince's things to the thrift shop?"

"Yes. We checked the pockets. Most were empty except for scraps of memos, which I saved for you. I also have a box for you of some items that I found in the closet that seem to be related to the business."

"Thanks. Do you mind if I take a quick look at the contents now?"

"Not at all. They're in his office." Evelyn rose to follow Sal into the office.

"Did you find anything personal?"

"No. But, I was hoping to find an address book."

"Which might contain Madison's telephone number and address."

"I was thinking that when I mentioned the box. It might be a good idea for you to check before Danni does," Evelyn suggested. "She might not like what she finds."

Sal nodded. "She already suspects that Vince was keeping a mistress. I'd sure like to know if Madison was the woman, and if she truly was more than a friend to Vince."

"I'd bet on it."

"This whole affair could open a can of worms in settling the estate. You didn't go through his desk or business files, did you?"

"No. I thought you might want to do that."

"I'll get to it right away."

CHAPTER 11
THE LOCK

Eddie hadn't seen Danni since the memorial service except for once, just a few days afterward, when he'd stood out on the beach in near freezing temperatures trying his best to catch a glimpse of her with her girlfriends, who were all huddled around the fire pit drinking what he supposed were hot toddies.

He wasn't due at her home for another week. The lawn was immaculate, the repairs done. He wanted to see her, talk to her. Tiffany had let him down, but he didn't think Danni would. If only she needed something repaired…something of urgency. A wide grin split his handsome face. A lock! A breach in security!

Eddie waited until after midnight, when the women would be asleep. He gathered his supplies and tools together and drove to Danni's home. It was a new moon tonight, darker than usual, so he needed a flash light. Shining it on the path so he wouldn't trip, he made his way to the side door, the one with the outdoor shower that everyone used when they came in from the beach. The cold wave had passed and it was warmer now…in the mid-70s. That should work to his advantage. Someone would take a walk on the beach, maybe even wade in the water, and walk up to rinse their feet off before entering the house. They would find the lock to the door broken, or the door wide open.

A dim light shone from the kitchen. The surface light of the stove had probably been left on so that the girls wouldn't trip if they got up at night for a snack or water. He shrugged his shoulders, put on his gloves, and went to work on the lock. Since it was one of the new locks with which he was familiar, he picked it, opened the door, unscrewed the door knob from the inside, and left it hanging. He noticed no one had ever installed a dead bolt, more than likely because the property had a security alarm. He closed the door quietly, turned, and went back down the path.

A high pitched shriek sounded. One of the girls.

Eddie ran back down the path to his truck, a slow smile appearing on his face. Not hesitating, he started it and sped off. Danni would be calling him in the morning.

CHAPTER 12
REPAIRS

"Where's your gun?" Vivian asked.

"I don't have one."

"What?"

"I don't have one. We have never had guns in the house," Danni said, punching 911 into her cell phone.

"Sweet Jesus!"

"Did someone try to break in?" Evelyn asked, wandering into the kitchen.

"Looks like it," Vivian continued.

"I'll call the police. They'll be here soon," Danni said, moving to the door.

"Don't open the door," Evelyn said. "He may still be there."

"Oh, my God. The door knob…it's ready to fall off!"

"Don't touch it, Danni," Vivian warned.

"Why don't you have a dead bolt on the door?"

Danni shrugged her shoulders. "I don't know. It never seemed important. It just leads to the outdoor shower."

"And on down to the beach," Vivian added.

"We have a security alarm."

"Which you never use," Evelyn said. "You probably need to be more careful now that everyone knows that a beautiful, wealthy widow lives here alone."

"You're right. I should use the alarm. I will from now on."

"Sam and I always check the doors twice. He's a doctor, and often has prescription medicines in his case at home."

"Of course. You would be more security conscious."

"I'll need to call Eddie first thing in the morning to repair the lock."

"Who's Eddie?"

"My new gardener and maintenance man."

"Will he come out right away?" Evelyn asked.

"I'm sure he will, especially if it's an issue of security."

"What will we do tonight?"

"I don't think he will come back...not after Vivian's piercing scream. We can't lock that door, but we can place a heavy chair in front of it and lock our bedroom doors," Evelyn said.

The police came and left. Danni filed a report. There were no prints on the knob, only those that were supposed to be there; Danni's, her guests', and her employees'.

Eddie arrived shortly after Danni called in the morning, to replace the lock and add a dead bolt. After he'd secured the door, he met all of Danni's friends, sat down, had breakfast with them, and listened to their stories.

CHAPTER 13
CURIOSITY

Pete sat in front of Madison's laptop. Pulling his favorite search engine up, he typed in Danni Giardini and clicked Find. Within seconds, a number of investigative site options popped up. He clicked on one he had successfully used before and entered her name, city, and state she lived in.

For a minimum amount of $39.95, he was able to obtain her maiden name, birth date, all phone numbers, marriages, divorces, relatives, neighbors, property ownership, small claims, judgments, bankruptcies, and liens. He took out his credit card, paid, sat back, and waited a few minutes for the results.

It was no surprise to him that she'd only been married once and had no judgments, bankruptcies, or liens against her. Neither, however, did she own any property in her own name or jointly, with the exception of the mansion and the Ferrari. He shrugged his shoulders. More than likely, the balance of the assets were all held in the name of the company. What did it matter? He'd done well and had money of his own. He didn't need or want hers. But he'd known both men and women to kill for much less than a Ferrari and a mansion.

After he'd read all of the information, he was satisfied that Danni was an honest and sincere woman, as well as the woman of his dreams. He rolled his shoulders, rubbed the back of his neck, shut down the computer, and rose. He needed to get out of the studio, breathe fresh air, and fish. He set out for the marina in Jupiter, where he docked the cruiser that he'd purchased from Vince last year. A couple of hours later, he gave up fishing for the day and headed toward the Del Rey Marina, which he thought was within jogging distance of Danni's home.

It was further than he'd counted on, and by the time he'd jogged by her home, he was hot and perspiring. Wiping his face with a hand towel that he'd tucked into his shorts, he stopped for a moment. As he stood there he noticed the architecture and lush landscaping that surrounded the property...tall palms, sea grape trees, bougainvillea, and Australian pines, which although beautiful, were messy and not native to Florida. He wondered why Vince hadn't had the pines replaced. Most locals didn't like them.

A black Porsche sat in Danni's circular driveway, along with the loaner from the body shop. She wasn't alone. He wondered who was with her. Could he find the home from the beach?

Pete continued his jogging and headed to the franchised hotel. He hadn't been to the lodging for years, not since it had been remodeled. Five or six years ago, a tropical storm and four hurricanes had ripped through Florida, destroying most everything in their paths, including the hotel. That had been before Madison had moved into the house on the intercostal, where she lived now. The house, like the hotel, had been rebuilt.

Walking through a breezeway to the pool area, Pete stopped, put some money in a Coke machine, and sat down in a chair to drink it. When he'd finished, he tossed the can into a nearby waste container and continued down to the beach. After jogging a half mile or so, he passed Danni's home. To his surprise, it wasn't protected by a fence or surrounded by landscaping for privacy.

There was a small sand dune, but still, it would be a short walk to the wooden steps and onto a veranda where the pool faced the Atlantic.

Suddenly, Pete's heartbeat jumped when he noticed Danni walking out onto the terrace carrying a tray. More than likely she intended to have a late breakfast near the pool. He turned and walked back to the hotel, not wanting her to see him.

***

Danni set the tray down on the table, sat, and took a sip of apple juice. Smearing the hot biscuit she'd placed on a small china dish on the tray with butter and honey, she took a small bite and gazed out to sea. After she'd finished her light breakfast, she read the Palm Beach Post from cover to cover, then set it down and rose from where she was sitting. She strolled over to the pool and dove in. After a few laps, she stepped out, dried off, laid down on a nearby chaise lounge, and opened a novel.

When she came in from the pool area, she showered, dressed, and went to the office to file papers that Sal had piled up on his desk. By five-thirty she decided she'd done enough work for the day and was ready to quit. Locking up, she decided to run some errands before going home. On the way back to her house, she stopped by the dry cleaners, the grocery, and finally the post office to pick up her mail. Perusing the mail, she sighed when she saw there was nothing of any importance there. The last stop reminded her how tired of being alone she was.

When she arrived home, she pulled into her driveway, parked, and broke out into a smile at what she saw.

"Sal?" she called out as she hurried into the office.

"Just a second, Danni. I just need another minute to put these files back."

"I'm so glad you're still here," The corners of her lips tilted up. "On the way back I stopped by the grocery and picked up a couple of T-bone steaks. Would you like to stay for dinner?"

"I can't think of anything I'd like more."

"Then I'll start up the barbecue. Would you like a glass of wine while we are waiting? A Cabernet?"

"You bet. I've been working in Vince's home office here for hours."

"By the way, did you notice the cruiser out there about three hundred feet off shore? It looks a bit like Vince's."

"Yes. I noticed it earlier. It's been going back and forth. It's probably just a sightseer or an angler. Many boats look alike. It's beautiful, but I know it isn't Vince's."

"How do you know that? Did he sell it?"

"Yeah, about a year or so ago."

"Did it belong to the company?"

"No. The title was held in Vince's name."

***

Over dinner, Sal briefly touched on a couple of out of state opportunities that he'd recently been informed of. "Just as soon as we have everything involving the settlement of Vince's estate resolved, I'll be going to Texas to check out the real estate market."

"If you're going to Austin, I'd love to go with you," Danni said. "I haven't seen my aunt for some time now."

"That would be great. I'll be looking at some land in the hill country and around Lake Travis."

"Are you thinking of starting a development around the lake?"

"Maybe. I can't really say until I check it out. From what I've heard, Austin is booming. On another matter, I've been overloaded with work lately. I'm going to need to replace Vince as soon as possible. I'm hoping that you will consider taking over his job responsibilities."

"Do you think that I could?" she asked, stunned by the

unexpected turn of their conversation.

"There's not a doubt in my mind," he replied, smiling.

Chapter 14
The Prowler

After Sal left, Danni cleaned up the kitchen, showered, slipped into her pajamas, and opened the sliding glass window that led to the patio facing the beach. She loved to listen to the sound of the waves crashing onshore. She turned away, plumped the pillows up, and crawled into bed. Drawing the sheet over her, she opened the novel she'd been reading. Within a half hour, she'd fallen asleep.

She slept fitfully, tossing and turning. *Wake up. You forgot to close and lock both sliding glass doors.* She rolled over and fell off the bed. Awakened, she recalled her dream and got up quickly from the floor. She slipped into her robe and went over to close and lock the sliding glass window in her bedroom. Then, moving barefooted through the large home that was well lit by nightlights, she checked the sliding glass door that led to the veranda off the great room. It was ajar. Concerned, she glanced at the well-lit pool and then to the palms and shrubbery near the side. She blinked. Her hand covered her heart when she saw a tall, slender figure step to the side of the shell path that led to the house from the beach. Her heart skipped a beat. *Someone's out there.* If it hadn't been for the dream and falling out of bed like a two-year-old child, someone could have entered her home, and more than likely would have. She closed the sliding door tightly and locked it. Moving from room to room, she checked all of the other windows and doors. Two were unlocked, but not open. She locked them, then set the alarm. She hurried back to the bedroom and locked the door behind herself.

What if he came back later? Her friends had already left. Sal had left hours ago. She was there alone here in the house. She'd heard that sliding glass doors were easy to enter. Vince wasn't coming back. Not ever. Even though she was angry and disappointed in him, her eyes filled with tears as she moved to pick up the house phone on the nightstand to call the police.

"Do you want us to bring the dogs?"

"Yes."

"Do you have a firearm in the house?"

"No," Danni replied.

"Good."

Good? For who? For them, maybe. And for the prowler, but not for me.

"Stay in your room. Make sure the door is locked. We're on our way."

Not long after her call, the police came with dogs.

"Whoever was here earlier has left, but it seems clear that they have come and gone from the beach, but not by boat."

"The rip currents here are strong. No one docks their boats or anchors near here."

"They could have come from anywhere. He might have driven to Highland Beach and parked either at the hotel or the lot across from it, and then walked down the beach."

"Maybe. But, I saw a boat earlier today cruising slowly by, back and forth, in view of the house."

"They may have docked it up the way and jogged down. There's no way of knowing." The officer looked at her a moment and frowned. "Have you received any strange phone calls lately?"

"No. Mmm. Well, yes. A couple of hang ups and 800 calls."

"Have you met anyone new, anyone that might fit the prowler's description?"

"No one who would prowl around my place."

"Are you sure? What about new employees? A new pool man? Maintenance man? Or maybe a new gardener?"

"I did hire a new gardener recently. My regular gardener quit just after Vince left on his trip."

"What does he look like?"

"Eddie's tall; maybe 6'1, tan, rail thin, sandy hair...sun bleached, medium brown mustache, kind of sun bleached too. His eyes are light brown, almost the shade of tea. He's been a real help to me. I don't have a maintenance man. Vince could fix anything. Now that Vince is gone, Eddie's been fixing things, replacing light bulbs, whatever I need. You know my cathedral ceiling is very high. Even with a ladder, I couldn't replace the bulbs or the batteries in the smoke alarms."

"Nor should you."

"When I'm home," Danni said, "I always make a sandwich for Eddie for lunch."

"Do you have lunch with him?"

"When I'm not busy. I've gotten to know him fairly well."

"So, you don't believe he should be considered a person of interest?" the officer asked.

"No. Not at all."

"What's his last name?"

"Haywood."

"Is he from this area?"

"No. He recently moved to Pompano Beach from Ft. Myers. He told me he drives back over once or twice a month to see his girlfriend."

The officer nodded. "Did you check his references?"

She nodded. "Yes, but only one. I wasn't able to reach the other woman. I think I had the wrong number."

"What was her name?"

"Tiffany something. I don't remember her last name, but it's on his application."

"What about personal contacts? Someone who may have been in your home that you've recently met?"

"I've met many new people lately, especially at Vince's memorial service and at the memorial party that was held at my home afterwards."

"Of course. You would have. We don't have the resources to check on everyone. Just be sure to keep your doors and windows locked and your alarm on at night. Call us right away if you have any other incidents."

"Thank you, Officer. I will. Wait a second." She recalled something." Later that night, I noticed someone had picked the lock, taken it apart, and then left it in pieces and fled. My maintenance man, Eddie, whom I mentioned earlier, came out the next morning and replaced the lock. He told me that if the lock hadn't been picked as I'd told him, he would have said that it might have broken due to the unusually cold weather that we've had lately. While he was here fixing it, he also installed a dead bolt."

"Good. From now on, use both."

Chapter 15
Self-Defense

Sal glanced up from the huge pile of work that had been waiting for him at the office. He realized he was going to need help, as he still hadn't gone completely through Vince's home office. He picked up the phone to call Danni, and when she answered he placed her on speakerphone.

"Danni! Hey! I'm so glad I was able to reach you. I was wondering if you might be able to come to the office again later today to fill in for me while I continue going through Vince's desk at your home. What time would be best for you?"

"Why don't you come by around one this afternoon? We can have lunch on the patio and afterwards, I'll go to the office."

"That would be great. See you then." Sal hung up. He worked for another two hours filing papers, along with Bobby.

"I realize you're going to be on your way back to school at the end of summer, Bobby, but I could sure use your help here in the meantime."

"I'll be glad to help, but while I'm still here, why don't you go ahead and hire an in-house bookkeeper, and maybe an office manager? That might make it easier for you after I leave."

Sal nodded. "I think I'll do that. Also, in case I hadn't mentioned it before, I'm thinking of starting up a development out of state."

Bobby turned and glanced at Sal. "Where?"

"In the Texas hill country; just outside of Austin."

"I've heard Austin's a rockin' town. I'd like to know more about it."

"I thought you wanted to stay in Florida."

"Hey, sometimes change is good."

"What about surfing?" Sal asked, knowing that was Bobby's passion, as well as a spiritual form of recreation for him.

Bobby shook his head. "After having surfed the Mexican pipeline, I realized that Florida doesn't have much surf; not even the Sebastian inlet. If I lived in Austin, I'd just catch a plane out to San Diego or to the Mexican pipeline to surf."

"That wouldn't bother you?"

"No."

"I'm glad to hear that." Sal rose and poured a cup of coffee. "Coffee?" he asked Bobby.

"Please. I've been about to fall asleep filing."

Sal carried two cups of steaming hot coffee back to the desk and stacked the papers neatly.

"What about Danni?" Bobby asked. "Do you think she would relocate?"

"I don't know, but I think it would be great for her." Sal didn't want Bobby to know, but he definitely thought she was being stalked. He didn't believe that the person who had walked up from the beach was either a fisherman or a drunk on his way home. Her stalker could be anyone who knew that Vince had been killed. "If Vince's estate hadn't been tight, held in trusts, Danni would be worth millions. Currently, since both the mansion and the car were titled jointly with right of survivorship, she is the owner of both…free and clear, without any liens."

Bobby whistled. "That's a small fortune in itself."

Sal nodded and glanced at his watch. Twelve forty-five p.m. "I'm going to lunch now, Bobby. When you're ready to quit for the day, go ahead and lock up.'

"I think I'll leave in a couple of hours. I'd like to do a little research on Austin; find out what, besides the music business and the university, keeps it going."

Sal grinned. "For one, it's the capital of Texas, and for another, it's a huge tech center."

***

Danni had just finished preparing Shrimp Louis when the doorbell rang. She washed and dried her hands and moved to open the front door.

"Sal! Come in. It's great to see you. I'm glad you could come for lunch."

His mouth turned up as he hugged her. "Count on having dinner with me tonight, too."

"That would be a pleasure. I'd enjoy your company. I'm not looking forward to being alone here tonight."

Sal's brow went up. "What's wrong?"

She related the story about the prowler and the police coming out to investigate.

"You need a dog."

"Unfortunately, I can't have a dog. I'm allergic to them. They make me itch."

"There are hypoallergenic dogs. You might seriously consider owning one."

"I didn't know there were hypoallergenic breeds. What are they?"

"Well, one of my favorites is the schnauzer. They make great guard dogs too, by the way. Another is the Maltese and the bichon frees, as well as the poodle. I know someone who has some miniature schnauzers for sale. There are two females and two males left."

"Are they housebroken?" Danni asked.

He laughed. "They're only two months old, but schnauzers are quite intelligent. I don't think they would be difficult to train."

"What about shots, and other things dogs need?"

"They've had their shots and have been dewormed."

"No one would be afraid of a puppy."

"True, but you just need an extra set of ears in the house. Don't you own a gun?"

"I wish I did. I would have felt much safer with one last night. To tell you the truth, I've never owned a gun, nor have I ever shot one."

"You're kidding. Vince didn't give you a gun or teach you to shoot, yet left you alone all these years while he was away on business?"

"I've never had any problems until recently."

"It's time you learned how to defend yourself. We're going shopping for a handgun. Then we'll do some target shooting. By this time next week, you will be able to handle a revolver, or maybe even a semi-automatic pistol."

"I would feel safer."

"Is lunch ready?"

She nodded. "I think you will like it."

"I'm sure I will."

"Would you like to have lunch on the veranda?"

"Sounds great."

"Today's Wall Street Journal is on the umbrella table if you would like to browse through it while I set lunch on a tray."

"Thanks."

***

Danni moved into the kitchen. While she was setting their lunch on a tray, the phone rang.

"Hello."

The caller remained silent.

"Hello?"

Silence.

"Hello?"

This time there was a long silence, then a heavy sigh.

An ominous sense of impending danger sent chills up her spine. She gathered her narrow brows together and hung up.

Placing their lunch on a tray, she carried it out to the veranda, wondering who the caller had been.

"Let me help you," Sal offered, getting up to take the heavily laden tray from her.

"Thank you."

"No problem. This looks great. Did you know that Shrimp Louis is one of my favorites?"

Danni couldn't contain her smile. "Yes. We're also having Key Lime pie for dessert."

"What a treat! I heard the phone ring. Was it anything important?"

"I don't know. It was odd. There was someone on the line, but they remained silent and then hung up. It gave me the creeps."

Sal drew his heavy brows together. "This doesn't sound good, especially in view of your recent prowler."

"I know. I've been thinking about it. Everyone in the Miami/ Palm Beach area who reads the newspapers knows that Vince was killed and that I'm a widow now."

"With that in mind, I would be careful trusting anyone new in your life."

"I'll take that to heart."

"I don't think it's a good idea for you to stay here alone, at least not until you have a dog and are able to defend yourself."

"I have an alarm system."

"Which you often forget to set, right?"

"Well, yes, but I've never had any problems until last night."

"After dinner tonight, come home with me. You know I have a guest room. You can lock the bedroom door if you want."

"Thanks, Sal, but I think you're making too much out of all of this."

"I don't think so. I have a gut feeling about this, and it's not good."

"To change the subject, I've been thinking, as much as I love this house, I've decided I'd like to sell it. It's too large for one person. A cute little condo would be so much better."

"Great idea."

"I think I'd like a place in a security-gated area."

Her cell phone rang. She picked it up, looked to see who was calling, and smiled. "Lainey! I was just thinking about you this morning. Yes! I'd love to come up. Sal's here. Let me check and see if it's okay with him. We've had a lot of work to catch up on."

Sal grinned. "When?"

"This evening. They want me to stay a couple of days. Can you spare me?"

Sal laughed. "Yes, of course, I can spare you. You can leave early. About five. We'll have dinner and transfer your personal things to my place when you come back."

"Okay. I'll be there around eight or eight-thirty."

"You'll be safe there." Sal was smiling as he spoke.

CHAPTER 16
THE STRANGER

Pete had docked at the marina last night, and rose early to do some fishing. After cleaning and filleting several fish that he'd decided to keep, he froze all but one fillet, which he fried, along with homemade hash browns, for breakfast. Slicing a tomato, he placed it on the plate alongside the fish, except for one quarter of the tomato, which he popped into his mouth. Chewing it slowly, he poured a cup of hot steaming coffee and sat down to eat. When he was finished with breakfast, he cleaned the galley and decided to make a run by Danni's house before he headed back up the intra-coastal to Madison's home.

Cruising as close to shore as he could safely do, he silently swore to himself when he saw a tall thin man in a pair of worn jeans and a work shirt on the veranda. *Who the hell is that? Someone who works for her? It sure isn't Catalano.*

After he arrived at Madison's, he pulled the boat in and docked behind the house on the intra-coastal. He went up to the garage apartment, took a shower, and cleaned up. After thinking of the man that he'd seen behind Danni's home, he sat down at a small desk in the living room and turned on the computer. First, he ran another search on Danni, just in case he'd missed something the first time. Huh! Why hadn't he noticed the last time that she was originally from New Orleans?

He smiled. Her voice…soft, with a slightly southern accent. No wonder. But he was still preoccupied with the identity of the person he'd seen on the veranda. Maybe JVS has added a new partner. He ran another search on JVS Building, Inc. However, he was unable to discover anything with regard to the man that he had seen. And so, he began to rationalize. Maybe he was nothing other than a gardener or a maintenance person who was working at the house.

CHAPTER 17
MADISON

Sal rifled through Vince's desk still looking for one thing…a private address book. After discarding and shredding most of the business files, he found copies of transactions which Vince had kept at the office. So far, he'd found nothing of any great importance.

Opening the center drawer of Vince's desk, he shuffled around and finally discovered a small red address book. Glancing through the book, he saw the name he was looking for…Madison Langley, and next to it, Madison's Books. Her telephone numbers, home address, and that of the bookstore were listed on the same page. He picked up the office phone and called the bookstore. The hours of operation were better than he had expected…nine a.m. to eight p.m. She must need money to open so early and stay open so late. He would soon know just how important Madison had been in Vince's life. He slipped the little address book into his briefcase and prepared to leave for the day. Locking up, he set the alarm just as Vince had long ago shown him.

Sal took Interstate #95 north to the Donald Ross exit. Turning right at the exit, he drove east until Donald Ross intersected with Highway 1. Turning north toward Tequesta, he headed toward the strip mall where the bookstore was located. He parked his black Porsche just a few doors down from Madison's Books, stepped out of the car, locked it, and walked briskly into Madison's Books.

Entering the shop, he stopped for a moment and stared briefly at the woman behind the counter, who was ringing up merchandise for a customer. The first thing he noticed was that her auburn hair was shorter, yet similar in style and color to Danni's. She appeared to be about the same age. Other than her nose and the shape of her face, he could have sworn at first glance that she was Danni's twin. When she stepped out from behind the counter, he noticed that she was pregnant and was not wearing a wedding ring.

"May I help you, sir?" she asked, glancing up. "You seem to be lost."

"No, I'm not lost, but this is the first time I've been in your bookstore. Perhaps you can help me. I'm...ah...looking for the mystery section."

She smiled, a beautiful smile made even more so by her dimples. "The mystery novels are in the shelves against the back wall. If you'll excuse me for a moment, I'll be right back to help you."

He recalled how Vince had always had good taste in women, and began to wonder if the child that Madison was carrying was his. Did she know that her lover, if that's what Vince had been to her, had been killed in a plane crash?

"Are you looking for a novel by a particular author?" Madison asked, appearing at his side.

"I have several favorite mystery writers. But before we do that, I'd like to speak with you about something else. I'm Sal Catalano, and it's about Vince Giardini, my former partner and I believe, a friend of yours."

She blanched. "Let's sit down on one of the sofas in the

reading area and talk." Leading him to a sofa, she asked, "Would you like coffee, tea, or perhaps a glass of wine?"

"A glass of wine, please." He sat down on the sofa. "You will have one too, won't you?" He was going to need it, and so would she.

"Red or white?"

"A Cabernet or a merlot, if you have it, would be nice."

"We'll have my favorite, Cabernet, then." Madison returned to the sales desk, reached under the counter, and returned to where Sal was sitting with two wine glasses, napkins, a wine bottle opener, and a bottle of Cabernet on a silver tray. Setting the tray down on the coffee table in front of the sofa, she asked, "You wouldn't mind opening the bottle, would you?"

"Of course not." Sal picked up the bottle from her, removed the cork, and poured two classes of wine for them.

"Thank you. Sometimes I have a problem with the corks. Mr. Catalano, about our mutual friend...my cousin, Peter Langley, told me he'd read somewhere of an accident he believed that Vince was in. Is he all right? I've been anxious to hear more."

Peter Langley? "Then we definitely need to talk. I'm presuming that you didn't know how to reach me, or what my business relationship was to Vince. I would have been more than happy to speak with you."

"No." She paused and set the glasses down on the table in front of the sofa. "I didn't know where to contact anyone connected with Vince, other than by calling the office of JVS Development, and I wasn't comfortable doing that."

"I'm sorry. I don't exactly know where to begin. First of all, let me start by telling you that it's a pleasure to meet you. I'm sorry that Vince didn't introduce us earlier, or at least tell me about you."

"It would have been awkward." Madison took a sip of her

wine.

"I have known Vince for most of my life, so please don't feel uncomfortable with me."

"You don't seem to be the type of man that I would feel uncomfortable with. I am so glad that you stopped by." Madison set her wine glass back on the table, then ran her fingers through her hair, pushing it back from her face. "It is a pleasure to meet one of Vince's good friends. Now, please tell me about the accident."

Sal relayed everything he knew about the crash, including the stop in Albuquerque and the possibility that Vince could have survived. "No one has heard from him that I know of."

"Neither have I." Madison paused and drew her fine brows together. "What do you think happened?"

"I don't know. They found his watch at the crash site, the one with his initials on the back."

Madison sighed. "He always wore that watch."

"Yes, he did. Because of that, we've presumed that he died in the crash. I am sorry to have to tell you this, but a memorial service was recently held for him at St. Lucy's Catholic Church on Highlands Beach." Sal rubbed the back of his neck. *Damn, I hate having to inform this lovely woman of Vince's death.*

Madison took a long sip of Cabernet and choked. Her eyes filled with tears. "Excuse me, please. I just swallowed wrong, and I need a glass of water. I'll be back in a moment."

Sal ran his fingers through his thick, dark, wavy hair. *Damn! Vince should have told me that he had a mistress.* This was no casual affair. Hell, Sal, himself, had had relationships with many woman, but he'd never settled down. To this date, the only woman he'd ever loved had married his best friend. However, neither Vince nor Danni had known that. Once he'd known that Vince was interested in Danni, he'd backed off because he hadn't thought that she was serious about him. That had been the biggest mistake he'd ever made. Who knows? She might have chosen him instead of Vince had she known she had other options.

He was afraid that Madison was pregnant with Vince's child. Since he was the executor of Vince's estate, he was going to need to ask. So far, he'd been able to delay the reading with the attorney, saying that he didn't believe that Vince would have re-boarded the plane. The possibility couldn't be ruled out, so he wanted to wait a week or two more before Vince's will and trust were read.

***

"I'm sorry." Madison walked back into the reading room and sat down on the sofa next to Sal. "I didn't realize that Vince had been killed. What a shock."

Sal nodded. "It's hard to believe, I know. From all of the information we've gathered, he was on board the aircraft that crashed in the Rockies."

She shook her head in denial. "My God! What a horrible way to die."

He nodded. "I agree. I can't imagine what it would be like to be a passenger on a plane that was going down."

"It's too terrifying to think about."

"Madison, I know this is a delicate question, but would you mind telling me what your relationship was with Vince?"

"He was the love of my life. I didn't know he was married until Pete, my cousin, told me. I had hoped to marry him, and would never have had a relationship of any kind with him had I known of his marital status. But, I didn't know or even suspect. We had a very physical relationship. I'm carrying his baby."

Sal grinned broadly, his suspicions confirmed. "Girl or boy? Vince always wanted a child. Unfortunately, his wife couldn't have children."

"They tell me that it's a girl."

"Vince would have been so excited. He didn't know, did he?"

"No. I believe I must have become pregnant in October or November. I wasn't showing much the last time I saw him. He thought I'd gained a little weight." The corners of her mouth turned up in a lovely smile.

"So, you're expecting in July?"

"Or late June maybe." She shook her head and her eyes filled with tears. "You're being so kind. Is his wife a friend of yours?"

"Yes. In fact, I met and dated her long before she met Vince."

"Life certainly has its twists and turns." Madison reached for her glass and took another sip of wine.

"Some wonderful; some miraculous, some nightmarish."

"I could do without the later." Madison was quiet for a moment, and then said, "Mr. Catalano, I want you to know that I will never ask for anything, not for myself nor for my child. I've never asked for anything from Vince."

"Thank you. That's extraordinary of you. Please call me Sal. Everyone else does. I don't believe if Vince had known about the child, he would have left you in the lurch, so to speak. Having met you, I'm sure he cared very much for you. However, if you will excuse me, I need to leave now, but I'll be back in touch with you next week. In the meantime, feel free to call me." He reached in his pocket and handed her his business card.

***

When Sal left the bookstore, he went directly to his car and headed north on Highway 1. Pulling into a gas station, he glanced into the address book again. After he'd filled the gas tank and purchased a bottle of water, he continued up Highway 1 to the address of Madison's home. Just before he reached the Martin County line, he came upon a modest-sized pale green split-level frame house with a garage apartment, which rested just yards from the Intracoastal Waterway. A small fishing boat was docked there. Charming, though dangerous during the hurricane season, it was a perfect spot for an artist or a fisherman, but not for a single mother with an infant or a young child.

CHAPTER 18
VISITING FRIENDS

When Danni arrived at Lainey and Running Deer's townhouse, Evelyn and Thomas were both there. After they visited for a while, they took a walk up the beach and had cocktails at a beautiful restaurant and lounge on the Atlantic Ocean. After dinner, they walked back to Lainey's.

The following morning, Danni awoke early. Sitting at a table for two in the Florida room, she took a drink of the strong, hot coffee that Lainey had brewed moments earlier. The clouds were low, golden and orange as the sun rose over the Atlantic.

"Good morning, Danni." Running Deer set his cup of coffee on the table and sat down in the other chair. "Beautiful, isn't it?"

"I love watching the sunrise over the sea. I don't think I'd like to live anywhere else but Florida."

Running Deer smiled and said, "The most important thing about where you live is the people you love and that love you. You can be happy any place as long as your heart and mind are in the right place. God's paintings, sunrises and sunsets, are beautiful everywhere."

"I suppose you're right. But, you must admit that our Florida sunsets are breathtaking."

Running Deer nodded. "You must visit us in Arizona soon.

The sunsets in Sedona will surprise you with their mystical beauty."

"I would love to."

"Then why not come back with us?"

"Sal is planning to check out the possibility of beginning a development near Austin. I'll be going."

"Isn't that where your aunt lives?"

"Yes. I'm really looking forward to the trip. I haven't seen Jazzy in a long time. She's more like a sister to me than an aunt. You know, or maybe you don't, that we had a band together when we lived in New Orleans."

"A band? Like in a blues band?"

Danni laughed. "Exactly. I sang and danced my way down Bourbon Street. Well, not literally, but in the clubs."

Running Deer's handsome Native American face split into a wide grin. "And in Austin, what does your aunt do?"

"She owns Jazzy's on Sixth."

"A blues club?"

"Of course. She still sings, dances, and plays a mean piano."

Running Deer smiled. "You're going to have a memorable trip; one that you will never forget."

"I hope Sal finds what he's looking for. He's been down since Vince's reported death."

"Reported death. That's an odd way to phrase it."

"I don't think Vince is dead."

Running Deer was silent.

"All right. You're a shaman. I know that you're psychic, but you're not saying a word."

"Why don't you think so?"

"The truth is, we weren't getting along well. I think that he took this opportunity to begin his life over again...with someone else. Some people do that."

"I don't think that's what happened, but right now, you have other issues."

"That's true. I have a prowler, and I think I'm being stalked. I'd like to sell my house and find a cute little condo with security, either on the beach or on the intracoastal."

"Have you placed your home on the market yet?"

"Not yet. I'm still considering. The market's not good."

"No. It's not. But I think you can sell your home anyway... that is, if it's priced right. Why don't you go ahead with this? Begin packing up your things and preparing your home to market. You might stay with Vivian and Sam, maybe Sal if you're comfortable with him, until you leave for Austin. That way, the boxes and all of the inconvenience of moving won't bother you so much."

"Maybe I will."

"Then do it. Not only to avoid living in a mess, but also, if you are being stalked, you are in danger in your home, and it can only become worse."

"I'll think about it."

Running Deer sighed.

CHAPTER 19
BREAK IN

Danni carried the remainder of her clothes in from the guest bedroom closet. She folded and packed the ones she wanted with her in suitcases. The others, mostly old winter clothes which she'd hardly ever worn, she folded, stacked, and placed in boxes for storage. She was still living in her home and hadn't followed Running Deer's advice. There was too much work left to do.

Nearly finished, all she had to do now was to check in the garage for items that needed to be disposed of. Moving into the garage, she noticed a small dusty olive green duffel bag resting on a shelf. Vince had always carried it to the gym with him and often left it in his car. Removing it from the shelf, she set it down, wiped it off, and unzipped it. Inside was a pair of his swim trunks, his spare pair of sunglasses, suntan lotion, deodorant, two beach towels, and a woman's yellow polka-dot thong bikini…size eight. She gasped. *I wear a size four or six. Where did these come from? I've never worn a size eight, and I hate polka dots!*

She remembered what the clerk had said at the hotel in Palm Beach. "You've lost weight." This was proof that Vince had been cheating. She stuffed the items back into the duffle bag, zipped it back up, and tossed it into a corner where the trash sat. Mumbling some choice words not fit for anyone's ears, she turned and went back into the house.

She'd been right. Vince had had a mistress. Had Sal known? Trembling with anger, she went back into the house and punched in Sal's number on the house phone. No answer. If Sal had known, he wouldn't have told her. For one, he wouldn't want to hurt her in any way. Secondly, Sal had been a loyal friend to Vince.

Who was the woman? She would find out. Had she been innocent? Had she been one of the many single women in the United States that married men hit on, not advising them of their marital status? Had Vince been in love with her?

Maybe the woman had seduced him, not only for his looks, but for his money. Maybe she'd fallen in love with him. She rubbed her forehead. As she always did when she was upset, she changed into a bathing suit and cover up. Grabbing a small tote, she tossed in a towel, a book, and a change purse. Setting out for the beach, she turned toward the hotel. A few minutes later, she was sitting at a table on the hotel patio facing the beach. She ordered a Long Island Iced Tea, finished it, and ordered another. Her ego had been badly bruised. If she'd had her cell phone with her, she would have called Pete. She needed company, and she needed to be loved.

The following day, Danni rose early. With a slight headache, she went directly to the office after carefully dressing and applying her makeup. She was not going to allow her recent discovery about Vince's betrayal depress her. She intended to put in a full day's work. By four o'clock, she'd sorted through all of the papers and filed them accordingly. A stack of mail from the past few days had accumulated, most of which were bills. Did Sal handle those, or was she expected to?

***

Sal walked into the office. "Hey, beautiful. I see you've been hard at work."

79

She nodded. "I've been here since early this morning. We've had a lot of mail pile up. I'm wondering if we have a bookkeeper or an accountant."

"Sure. Do you have something for him?"

"Bills."

"I'll handle those. We pay them, and then turn over the receipts to the accountant at the end of the month. It's not much work; however, I plan to hire a bookkeeper since we will be out of town for a while."

She nodded. "I'd like to talk with you about Vince. Do you have a couple of minutes?"

"Sure."

She cleared her throat.

Uh-oh. When she does that, it's something bad. "This is serious, isn't it?"

"Maybe."

"In that case, I think I'd like to have a beer or a glass of wine while we chat about it. Would you like something?"

"I haven't had an easy day, and its past four o'clock already. I think I'd like a glass of white zinfandel; maybe some cheese and crackers along with it. Sit down, Sal. I'll get the drinks and make a plate of appetizers. I need a break from sitting anyway. Will it be beer or a glass of wine for you?"

"I'll have a beer, thanks."

Danni excused herself and moved into the restroom to freshen up and wash her hands. Feeling better already, she moved into the small kitchen area and prepared a tray. When she moved back into the office, she arranged everything on a side table and handed Sal a beer and a couple of napkins.

She took a sip of wine. "I thought we had disposed of all of Vince's things, but I noticed his duffle bag in the garage yesterday. After opening it, I found some things of Vince's, along with a

80

polka dot bikini that I can tell you wasn't mine."

Sal took a long pull of beer.

"I don't think there is any doubt about the fact that Vince had had a woman on the side. I've thought so ever since the desk clerk at the Grand Duchess thought he'd seen me before. I hope that she was told about the accident. I don't know who she is or I would tell her myself."

Sal took a deep breath and expelled a deep sigh. "I found her name in an old address book of Vince's. In fact, I went to see her yesterday."

"You did? Why didn't you call me right away?" Not giving him the time to answer, she said, "Who is she? What's she like?"

"First of all, she didn't know that Vince was married. Secondly, she didn't know he'd been killed."

"Good grief! What a shock that must have been."

"More than you might think. I'm glad you poured a glass of wine for yourself. You may need it."

"What do you mean?"

He took another deep breath. "I don't know how you're going to take this, but she's pregnant with Vince's child. She'd hoped to marry him."

"Oh, my God! What a mess Vince made. Why didn't he use protection? Why wasn't he honest with her? Why didn't he tell her he was married?"

Sal held both hands out, palms up. "I don't know."

Danni cleared her throat. "This could create a problem with the estate."

"That was my first thought. But after talking with her, I don't think she will cause any trouble."

"Why not? She may need money to support the child."

"Yes, I suspect she will, but she expects nothing. I've given some thought to this and, if the child is truly Vince's, which can be proven by DNA tests, I'll make certain that both she and the child are treated fairly."

"That's the right thing to do, of course."

"That's kind of you to say, especially under these circumstances."

"You had nothing to do with this. Evidently, the woman is innocent as well. It's Vince that I'm furious with. This is so frustrating. I would dearly love to tell him what I think of him. I may be Catholic, but reincarnation makes perfect sense to me. I hope he receives the karma due him!"

Sal laughed. "Reincarnation or not, I don't believe we can get away with anything. He has a lesson to learn, and I'm sure he will."

"In hell or in purgatory."

"Or in his next lifetime."

"I just remembered something. What is the woman's name? It isn't Madison, is it?"

He nodded.

"Oh jeez. She's Pete Langley's cousin. She must have been Vince's companion when he stayed at the Grand Duchess Hotel in Palm Beach. She's the woman they mistook me for."

Oh, man. Vince must have checked them in as Mr. and Mrs. Giardini.

"She must look a lot like me."

"You could be twins. By the way, who's Pete? How do you know him?"

"You remember. He's the artist, a financial consultant that I met in Palm Beach. I bought two of his paintings."

***

Sal drew his brows together. "That's right. I remember you telling me about him. I also remember the paintings that you brought home from the gallery in Palm Beach just after Vince was killed. He painted several of them, didn't he?"

Danni nodded. "He's a wonderful artist." She cleared her throat. She darned well wasn't going to tell him how she felt about Pete. They hadn't known each other long.

"How well do you know him?"

She avoided the question. "I'm having lunch with him tomorrow. He's bringing a couple of his new paintings down to a gallery in Boca."

"I'd like to meet him."

"Perhaps I can arrange it."

"Say, are you available now? I'd like to make a phone call, and if it's convenient with the owner, I'd like to look at some dogs with you. We can have dinner afterward."

"Sure, that would be fun." While he made the phone call, she picked up her handbag, went into the powder room, refreshed her makeup, and brushed her hair. Spraying a bit of perfume on, she walked out looking and feeling like a new woman.

"Are you ready, beautiful?"

"Absolutely. I need a break. The conversation we just had about Vince and his mistress has disturbed me more than I can say. For one, I had actually thought that he was still alive, living with his girlfriend, but what you've just told me rules that out."

***

It was late when she came home. Sal hadn't wanted her to stay there tonight. Not because of romantic purposes, but because he was concerned for her safety. He'd even offered her his spare room. Thinking of his concern, she checked all of the doors and windows before she went to bed. She awakened in the middle of the night to the beckoning call of the waves washing onshore.

She rose and slipped into a terrycloth robe that she often wore as a beach cover up. Peering out the windows that faced the patio leading onto the beach, she saw no one lurking about. She hadn't expected to. She didn't think the prowler would return, not after she'd called the police. Unlocking the sliding glass door that led to the patio, she followed the seductive call of the sea.

She stepped out into the night and moved onto the shell path that led down to the beach. Behind her, a rock tumbled down. She stopped and listened. Had she been wrong? Had there been someone hiding in the shadows? Was there someone behind her, watching? She'd been on the beach at night a million times before and nothing had happened. No one had bothered her. But, it was different now. She was alone and vulnerable.

Her instincts were screaming of danger that lurked nearby. A shiver raced up her spine. Her heart began to race. Another rock tumbled down. She turned and ran back up the path, glancing toward shrubbery near the pool and the house.

Once inside, she locked up tight, turned on soft music, and made a hot toddy, heavily laced with bourbon. A false sense of security assured her that it had all been her overactive imagination. What had happened before must have been a fluke.

Not quite ready to go back to bed, she made another hot toddy, then sat at the breakfast bar, sipped it, and glanced through a fashion magazine. When she returned to her bedroom, she crawled back into bed and was sound asleep in minutes.

Awakened near dawn by an uncomfortable sensation, a feeling that she was not alone, she opened her eyes and gasped. Too dark to see details clearly, she couldn't miss the tall, slender figure of a man wearing a ski mask over his face. He stood at the side of her bed looking down at her. Startled, she jumped up, gasped, and opened her mouth to scream. His hand clamped down over her mouth.

"Be quiet," he warned. "Don't scream. I'm not going to hurt you. Lie back down and stay there. I'm tired. I've been driving a long way and I have further to go. I just want to rest and lay down next to you for a while."

"No!"

His hand covered her mouth again. "I told you. Lie still. Don't try to call the police or leave. If you do, you'll be sorry."

Okay. Maybe I was wrong about not taking Sal or Running Deer's advice. What was I thinking? How strong and brave I am?

Danni was laying still, flat on her back, trembling, afraid to move. What did the man lying next to her want? Sleep? She didn't think so. Rape? Maybe. Murder? Who knows? *If he's telling the truth, he only wants to rest. But why in my house? In my bed?* She prayed and prayed that he would fall asleep. When he did, she would silently crawl out of bed and then make her way outside, the way the stranger had entered, through the sliding glass door.

How could she have possibly forgotten to lock it? She'd thought someone had been watching her. Maybe she had locked it and the intruder had by-passed the lock. It must be easy to do that or people wouldn't place wooden rods in the base, she reasoned. A half-hour later, she moved to turn over on her side, away from him.

"Don't even think about it." The intruder threw his arm over her, holding her down. "Go back to sleep. I'll be gone in the morning."

After you do what?

Danni didn't sleep; at least she didn't remember falling asleep. At dawn, she rolled over. Not a peep from the stranger. Looking over her shoulder, she saw that no one was there. She rolled out of bed. *He must be gone. But maybe not. Maybe he's in the bathroom or in the kitchen.*

She grabbed her handbag, which was on the chair next to the window, and ran outside through the half-open sliding glass door that he'd evidently entered through. She ran, stumbled on a sprinkler head, and fell face down on the wet grass. Pulling herself up off the ground, she didn't look back, but fumbled in her handbag for the keys. Grabbing them, she clicked the fob to unlock the car door. She ran for the car, opened the door, rushed in, and drove to the office with part of her nightgown caught in the door. Unaware that the gown was flapping in the breeze, she continued to drive down the street. When she arrived, she opened the car door, grabbed the strap of her handbag, hurried out of the car, and slammed the door shut. Clicking the fob to lock it, she ran to the office door. Still in a hurry, expecting the home invader to be right behind her, she unlocked the office door, slammed it behind her, and locked the door. Feeling somewhat safe now, she exhaled a deep breath and lay down on the sofa in the reception area.

***

Sal awoke early after a restless night. Showering and dressing in a pair of Chinos and a casual shirt, he stopped at a coffee shop for a quick breakfast and went to the office. When he stepped in, the first thing he saw was Danni, sound asleep on the sofa in an apricot-colored nightgown, which had crept up above her grass-stained knees. A corner of the gown was ripped. He moved to the closet, removed a light blanket, and covered her. She wasn't the only one who had ever slept on the sofa here, but she was the only one who had legs like that. Evidently she'd had a bad night, far worse than he. He wondered what had happened. Sal made coffee, poured a cup, and took it into his office.

***

Danni awoke to the fragrant scent of coffee. At first she didn't know where she was. She sat up and took note of her surroundings. What was she doing here, in the office? She panicked. The stranger. She remembered it all. She rose, wrapped the blanket around her, and moved into the ladies' room, where she splashed water on her face and washed and dried her hands and knees. After finger-combing her hair, she walked out and moved into the small area that contained a microwave, fridge, and coffeepot. Pouring herself a cup of hot, steaming coffee, she peeked into Bobby's office, then Sal's.

"Hey, beautiful! I didn't expect to see you here when I came in this morning. What happened to bring you to work so early, and in your nightie, too?"

Danni laughed and ran her hand through her hair. "I'm a mess, aren't I?"

"A beautiful mess. Want to tell me the story?"

"Oh my God! I was so frightened."

Sal drew his brows together. "Tell me." He listened without commenting as Danni related her experience. "You did the right thing. I don't know what else you could have done."

"There were things I never should have ever done, like telling myself that everything was all right, that the prowler wouldn't be back, like going out onto the patio and walking down the path, not to mention falling asleep with the alarm off."

"None of those things were a good idea, but the point is, you're all right. When you finish your coffee, we'll go over to the house together and call the police."

"That sounds good. I don't think I could go back to the house alone now, not knowing if the intruder is still there or not."

"Of course not. That would be foolish."

"I've never experienced anything like that."

"Why would you have? Home invasion shouldn't happen to anyone. Why don't you stay in one of my guest rooms, and we'll talk about what you would like to do. I have plenty of room. You're welcome to stay with me as long as you like."

"Thank you, Sal. That's very nice of you." Even though she'd turned him down before, she was now ready to accept his generous offer. "If you're ready, we can go to my house now. I'd like to shower and dress."

"Okay. I'm going to call the police and have them meet us there. Don't worry about what you're wearing. Just keep the blanket wrapped around you."

"He told me not to call the police."

"Who?"

"The intruder."

"Of course he did."

"He told me that I'd be sorry if I did."

"The bastard. He's the one who will be sorry if we ever find out who he is."

It was nearing ten a.m. by the time they pulled into Danni's drive. The police were already there. Danni relayed the story to them, leaving nothing out. While the police checked the home and made certain that the intruder had left, Sal and Danni waited outside.

"He's gone. There's no sign of anything. Nothing's been disturbed. You can go in now. Did he set off the alarm?"

"No. It wasn't on."

"Why not?"

"I woke up in the middle of the night and couldn't go back to sleep, so I went out to the patio and halfway down the path to the beach. Then I felt uneasy, turned around, and went back to the house. I locked up, but forgot to set the alarm."

"From now on," the officer advised, "do not go out onto your patio or for a walk on the beach in the middle of the night. Use your alarm. We've been out a couple of times. Something's wrong here."

No kidding. "Yes, sir. Thank you."

***

Once the officers had left, Sal's face brightened. "I have a great idea. Why don't you call a real estate person and list the house? I have some work to do in Vince's office here. While I'm doing that, pack your clothes in a couple of suitcases. I think it would be a really good idea if we leave the house to the realtors."

"I think you're right. In fact, I've already packed a couple of suitcases full of clothes, and some boxes for storage. I'd also like to remove my valuables, as well as the paintings."

"That's a good idea. Do that now, while I'm here. Will you need more boxes?"

"I don't think so," Danni replied. "Lainey and Evelyn picked up quite a few when they were packing Vince's things."

"Good. The sooner we're out of here, the better."

"It might be worthwhile to leave the furniture and sell it furnished, except for the antiques and special pieces. Wherever I go, I expect the house or condo that I choose will require different furniture."

Sal nodded in agreement. "I have another idea. I'd like to stage the largest model. Would it be all right with you if we place the furniture you would like to sell in it instead?"

"Yes. Even better."

"I'll call the guys to come over and pick it up then."

By late afternoon, the house was on the market and Danni was having cocktails with Sal in his penthouse overlooking the Atlantic. Whether she stayed at Sal's, caught a plane to Austin to visit Jazzy, or traveled halfway around the world, she was not going back to stay in her house one more night.

The next morning they went shopping for a firearm, a stun gun, and pepper spray. Danni stopped along the way to inquire about the possibilities of signing up for a self-defense class. A few weeks later, after purchasing a Browning nine-millimeter semi-automatic, she was on her way to becoming legally armed and dangerous. Target shooting had soon become one of her favorite hobbies, one that she was a natural at. As far as self-defense and taking men like Sal or Bobby down, it would be awhile before she was proficient enough to disarm either of them, or defend herself against them.

***

"I was with Danni yesterday." Bobby glanced at Sal. "I think someone was following us."

Sal took a deep breath. "I know. We've had calls at the office for her, too."

"I think she's still being stalked."

"She is."

"Who's that Pete guy that keeps calling her?"

"An artist that she met in Palm Beach. He's okay. Both Lainey and Running Deer know him."

"She has a luncheon date with him tomorrow. Did you know that?"

"Yes. I'd forgotten about it. Unfortunately, she needs to cancel it. I'd like you to drive over to Sarasota this afternoon with her and check on our project there. I think a week will do it. Stay at the club on Longboat. There's security there. I'll call now and make reservations."

"What about the luncheon with Pete?" Bobby asked.

"I'll call Danni. This is more important than her date." Sal picked up the office phone and punched in his home number. He was certain she was still there. Putting the call on speaker phone, he said, "Hey, Danni! We have a problem over in Sarasota. I'd like you to pack a bag and ride over with Bobby this afternoon. Plan on staying about a week. I realize that you are planning to have lunch with Pete, but I'd like you to cancel it. Tell him that you have an emergency, but do not, DO NOT…," he repeated, "tell him or anyone else where you are going."

"He'll want to know what happened and where I'm going to be staying. Why don't you want me to tell Pete where I am

90

going?"

"Someone was following you and Bobby yesterday, on top of all the other incidents that you've had. Don't worry about Pete. I'll have our secretary call and cancel your luncheon date."

"That's rude. Pete isn't following me, and he won't understand."

"If he doesn't understand, then he's not a friend, Danni. I need you in Sarasota. In fact, I needed you there yesterday."

***

Danni sighed. It was impossible to argue with Sal when he was insistent, just like it had been with Vince or even James when he'd been alive. "All right," she said, giving in. "I'll call him later and apologize. Just make sure that someone calls and cancels."

"Okay, beautiful. Bobby will be there to pick you up soon. Plan on going to Austin with me in a couple of weeks, too. Pack your jeans for Austin."

Danni smiled. "Now, that will be fun. I'll call Jazzy and let her know."

"Good. While you're in Sarasota, I'd like you to check out everything in our project that is for sale or for lease. If it needs to be refurbished, arrange it—do whatever it needs to move it."

***

An hour later, the secretary called. She wasn't coming in today…she had an emergency. Sal nodded, hung up, and forgot about canceling Danni's luncheon date with Pete.

CHAPTER 20
STOOD UP

Pete glanced around the restaurant. Danni hadn't arrived. He moved to the hostess and asked for their table, instructing the hostess to escort her to their table when she arrived. He waited for fifteen minutes, and then ordered a glass of iced tea. By the time a half-hour had passed, he decided something had happened. Either she'd been delayed at work or she'd had an accident. Unless she'd been suddenly stricken by the flu, and he was pretty sure she wasn't ill.

He took out his cell phone and punched in Danni's cell phone number. No answer. He left a message on her voice mail. She'd never given him her home telephone number. He'd tried to find it, but it was unlisted. He could call the sales office of JVS Builders, but he didn't want to do that. If she wasn't there, he didn't want any questions asked, nor did he care to speak to Catalano.

"Would you like to order, sir?" the waitress asked.

Pete glanced at his watch. He needed to be at the gallery in no less than an hour. He was hungry and couldn't wait any longer. "Yes, please. It seems the person I expected to join me is not going to be able to today."

"What would you like, sir?"

"I'll have a bean burger with lettuce and tomato, please."

"With fries, onion rings, or cottage cheese?"

"Neither. A mixed green salad with oil and vinegar on the side, please."

"Anything else?"

"No. Thank you."

By the time he'd finished his lunch, he was beginning to worry about Danni. He didn't think she was the type of woman who would stand him up. But then, maybe he was wrong. After his meeting with the manager of the gallery, he drove on home to Tequesta, changed his clothes, grabbed a rod, a bucket, bait, and set out for a late afternoon and evening of fishing. When he came in later, he checked his cell phone. Not a word from Danni.

Confused, his spirits were sinking. He could barely motivate himself. As he always did when he was down or confused, he turned inward toward his creativity. He painted for hours at a time. He forgot about lunch and dinner. About nine p.m., he made a peanut butter and jelly sandwich, drank a glass of milk, and went back to the easel until he could no longer hold his eyes open. He continued this schedule for the next few days. Finally, on the fifth day at sundown, he wandered out to the pier where his boat was tied up. Madison came out with a soda and a beer.

"What's wrong, Pete?" Madison asked, handing him the ice cold beer. "You've kept to yourself in the apartment for days now. That's not like you."

"I'm working on a painting."

She nodded. "Is that it? Then that explains it. You've haven't stopped by for days. I figured when I saw your SUV here that you would have dinner with me on Thursday, like you usually do."

"I'm okay, Madison."

"Right," she said with an edge to her voice. "And I'm not pregnant and unmarried."

"Okay. Your life's a lot more complicated than mine is, but

just think how much fun it's going to be to have a little baby girl around here!"

She grinned. "It is going to be fun. But what's up with you, Pete?"

He sighed. "Danni stood me up for lunch last week; didn't call to cancel or anything. I thought at first that she might have had an emergency. Now, I'm beginning to think that she's just doesn't like me."

Madison drew her fine brows together and studied her cousin a minute or so. She was quiet. "I don't think that's it, but you have a thing for her, don't you?"

He shrugged. "I thought she liked me. We just seemed to click, but maybe I'm wrong."

"I don't think so. Something must have happened that she couldn't call. Don't make a judgment call on this. Remember, she's going through a period of grief."

I don't know about how much grief she's feeling. She's angry and bitter because of Vince's affair with you. Cheating on Danni and not telling you that he was married was really a jerky thing to do. So was not using protection during sex. What were you thinking?"

"About not using protection...Vince didn't have a condom with him. I had a box of old ones in the drawer of my nightstand. He used those."

"Oh, jeez."

"Other than that, I have to agree with everything else that you said. However, no one's perfect. Maybe you need to take a break, Pete."

"That's a damned good idea. I think I'll go over to the studio on the other coast for a while."

Madison nodded. "That might be the best thing for you."

"Will you be okay?" Pete asked with a concerned expression

on his handsome face.

"Sure. I'm not expecting for a couple of months yet, not until mid-June at the earliest. Just be back by then, okay?"

"You can count on it."

Pete went back inside, packed, and began loading the SUV. He backed out of the driveway intending to go straight over to the other coast. When he came to I-95, he altered his plans and turned south, heading toward Highlands Beach. He had to see Danni, had to know if she was all right and why she'd stood him up. No one had ever done that to him. He'd been on his best behavior with her. He couldn't figure it out.

Her car wasn't parked in the driveway. The house was dark, and the porch lights weren't on. A For Sale sign had been erected in her yard. His heart fell. She was selling her home. He pulled in the driveway, took a pad of paper from the glove compartment, and searched for a pen. There wasn't one. So much for leaving a note. He shrugged his shoulders, stepped out of the car, and walked up to the front door. A lock box had been placed on it. She'd moved out. Now he was more worried than depressed. What had happened?

Returning to the SUV, he drove back onto Interstate 95 and headed north to Highway 80, which took him into the glades. When he reached Belle Glade, he stopped at a gas station, purchased a bottle of water and crackers to snack on, and filled up with gas, which he thought would take him to his destination without stopping again. By the time he reached Clewiston, he realized he'd over-extended himself. He was exhausted.

Pete stopped at the old historical Clewiston Hotel, hoping they would have a vacancy. He was out of luck…they were full. Getting back into the SUV, he rubbed his eyes. He could take a chance and sleep here in the parking lot, but how long would it be before security asked him to move? He couldn't think of a rest area between Clewiston and Ft. Myers. There were a couple of hotels ahead in Clewiston and some in La Belle, which wasn't far. But, what if they were all full? Better turn around to the rest area near the Miami Canal just to the east of Clewiston.

As soon as he saw it, he made a U turn, pulled in, and rolled to a stop near a picnic table. A large RV was parked nearby, and a pickup truck. Making certain that the car doors were locked, he scrunched down in his seat, closed his eyes, and slept until nearly dawn.

CHAPTER 21
EDDIE'S RAGE

Eddie couldn't get Danni out of his head. He thought of her day and night. The house was for sale...he'd seen the sign. She been frightened by him, and he knew she'd called the police when he'd told her not to. She didn't obey. She was just like all the others. He didn't think the house had been sold yet. There wasn't a sign indicating that it had. Even though he hadn't seen her recently, he figured that she must have still been living there. Where else would she go?

If she'd gone out and wasn't home yet, he'd wait. Then he'd teach her a lesson. It was dark, the phase of the balsamic moon with low-hanging clouds. No one would see him enter the home. He'd already been in the house, knew the layout, and how to by-pass the alarm. No one knew he'd worked for a security company. He never included it in his resume, mostly because he'd been fired from the company.

He moved up the lonely beach. When he reached the path, he barked out a harsh laugh. Someone had left the one of the sliding glass doors open, either Danni or the realtors.

When he entered the house, he walked silently through, noting the absence of furniture. Rage stormed through him. Moving down the hallway toward the bedrooms, he turned and smashed his fist through the wall. He'd find her if it took the rest of his life. When he did, he'd punish her or whoever had coaxed her into leaving. The guest bedroom door next to him was closed. He turned and hit it repeatedly with his fists until there was nothing left but sawdust.

He left Danni's house with revenge at the top of his list. Sal came to mind. And then the woman he'd trusted who had so recently told him that she loved him. She'd changed her phone number without telling him. He suspected she was seeing someone else on the side. She needed to be taught a lesson. He knew where to find her, and he needed to take care of her NOW.

CHAPTER 22
THE RENDERING

Danni and Bobby checked into the luxurious condo on Longboat Key near sunset. After she'd freshened up, she opened her handbag to retrieve her cell phone so that she could call Pete and apologize to him for not canceling their date personally. It had been rude for Sal to ask the secretary to do it. After she'd called Pete, she would call Sal to let him know that they had arrived. Shuffling around, she drew her brows together. The phone was missing. Maybe it had fallen out of her handbag and onto the seat or the floor of the car.

She took her keys, left the condo, took the elevator down to the parking lot, and walked to the car. After she'd thoroughly checked it, she threw her arms out to her sides, palms up.

"What's wrong, Danni?" Bobby asked, walking up to the car to unload more luggage from the trunk.

"I can't find my cell phone. I must have left it at the restaurant in Arcadia, or maybe in the ladies' room at the service station."

"We can call and ask," Bobby suggested.

"Okay, but if I left it either place, it's probably not there now."

"Probably not."

Danni went back into the condo, used the landline, and called both the restaurant in Arcadia and the service station in

Okeechobee. Neither place had found her cell phone. She waited for Bobby to return with the luggage.

"Did you find it?"

She shook her head. "Maybe I packed it."

Bobby grinned. "Unlikely, but here are your bags. I'll put them in your room. Uh…do you mind taking the one with the pink bedspread and curtains?"

She laughed. "No. That's fine."

An hour later, she'd unpacked; her clothes were hung, but there was no cell phone to be found. She sighed, moved to the phone in the bedroom, and called her service provider. So far, no calls had been made. She reported it lost and called Sal to advise him of their arrival and the loss of her cell phone. Placing him on speakerphone, she opened a bottle of water, sat down in a chair, and propped her feet up on the matching ottoman.

***

"I'm glad you and Bobby arrived safely. He'll pick up another cell phone for you tomorrow. This one will be in the company's name and will have an assigned company number."

"But, everyone has my personal number." Danni breathed out a sigh of sheer exasperation.

"That's just it. I'll bet that you've been receiving hang ups and weird calls on your cell, too."

"I have."

"You can call your close friends and advise them of your new number. But, don't give it to Pete, the gardener, or anyone else that you have met in the past six months, man or woman."

"Don't you think that's carrying it a little too far, Sal? I know you're worried about me and all, but—"

"You haven't heard the latest. The police called today. Your home was broken into and vandalized."

"Vandalized! But, we removed everything except for the

100

window coverings and appliances."

"Good thing. Someone broke in and punched in some walls in the hallway leading to your bedroom. The door to the guest bedroom was literally powdered. There's nothing left of it but splinters and sawdust."

"My God! It sounds as though the person was out of his mind."

"More than likely because you moved. They left through the sliding glass door in your bedroom."

"That's where the intruder entered the other night."

"The door was left open with the draperies blowing in the breeze. The realtor called the police."

"Do they know who did it?"

"No. There are hundreds of fingerprints in the house now. Think of the realtors, and the number of potential buyers that have walked through."

"I guess you're being prudent."

"I care about you, Danni. I don't want anything to happen to you. Is Bobby there?"

"Yes. Do you want to speak with him?"

"Please."

"I'll get him," Danni said, moving into the kitchen. "Sal would like to speak with you. He's on the speakerphone in my bedroom."

***

Danni poured a glass of wine and carried it out to the screened-in porch that overlooked the white sandy beach and the Gulf of Mexico. A crimson, orange, and gold sky reflected upon the calm waters of the Gulf. Sandpipers skittered along the shoreline while gulls dove for their specialties. Danni took a sip of the fine Cabernet and admired the beauty surrounding her.

***

The next morning, Danni rose early to take a jog on the beach. When she returned, she showered, dressed, and brewed a pot of strong coffee with chicory. After pouring a cup of coffee, she moved out onto the patio, sat down in a wicker chair, and began to read the morning paper.

"Aunt Danni. I didn't see you out here. When did you get back?"

"Not long ago. I just made coffee."

"Have you seen the morning paper?"

"Not yet. I just opened it and haven't read the entire front page yet. This is terrible!"

"Yeah. I read it earlier. A girl by the name of Tiffany Owens was killed, murdered actually. They believe she was picked up by some dude that she knew in a parking lot in Ft. Myers near her place of work. Someone saw her leave and get into an old white F250 pickup truck. Evidently, she knew the guy. When they found her body in a ditch near Ft. Myers, she'd been beaten to death and stabbed in the heart."

"'When last seen alive,' Danni read, "She was wearing a white-on-white sundress with lace trim. Her shoes, gold sandals with a moderate to expensive brand name, were found near her body. Her dress was bloody, the bodice ripped away and the skirt torn. She didn't have on nylons. Her panties, which were white lacy silk thongs, had been ripped off.' So, she had probably been raped or assaulted. From what I can tell by what she was wearing, she must have shopped at the better department stores, and had a sense of design and color."

"Anything else?"

"Though several of her acrylic nails had been torn and ripped off, it appeared that she had recently had a fill and a pedicure. So, we know that even though she may not have received a great salary at the store where she worked, she received some kind of second income somewhere, maybe from her boyfriend."

"Or from alimony, if she'd been married and divorced," Bobby added.

Danni drew her brows together. "What was her name again?"

"Tiffany Owens. She was about twenty-seven years old."

"That name sounds familiar. Where have I heard it before? Do they know who did it?" Danni asked. "It might not be the person who picked her up from work."

"They're looking for the dude in the artist's rendering on the front page. They say he's not wanted for murder, but that he is of interest to the police and is wanted for questioning."

Danni turned the newspaper back to the front page. She bit her bottom lip. "Holy smokes! This looks a little like someone I met just after Vince was killed. It can't be though. He lives on the other coast."

"Aunt Danni, it's only a couple of hours between coasts. What's this guy's name?"

"Pete. He's an artist and a friend of mine. But the rendering also resembles someone else even more closely. I know him."

"Maybe you should call the police."

"I don't know. Something's not quite right. And what would either of them be doing in this area?"

"Committing murder?"

Danni's hand covered her hammering heart. "No. I don't believe that. I think this is a case of mistaken identity. Wait a minute. I think I know who Tiffany Owens is."

"Who?"

"I'm not sure what Eddie's girlfriend's last name is, but I could swear it was Owens."

"Eddie? The gardener? He kind of looks like the guy in the artist's rendering."

She nodded.

"What's his last name?"

"Haywood."

"You'd better tell the police."

"I don't know. I don't want to give them false leads."

"Maybe he didn't kill her, but he may have seen something," Bobby suggested.

"Who saw this man who is 'of interest to the police,' and where did they see him?" Danni asked.

"A person in the shopping center saw the driver of the truck that picked her up."

"That doesn't mean he killed her."

"No. It doesn't."

"Who found her body?" Danni asked.

"A truck driver."

"Does he have a name?"

"Bubba Jackson…er, actually, Billy Bob Jackson."

"Billy Bob Jackson?"

"Right. That's what it says here," Bobby replied. "The police feel the person in the shopping center might have seen or heard something that would lead the police to find the murderer."

"I doubt it. The killer is probably long gone."

Bobby nodded. "You'd think so. But, Aunt Danni, you have an obligation to the soul that was murdered to help find her killer."

"Yes. I do."

"I've heard that murder victims often stay near the lower planes until their killers are found. The dead girl might haunt you if you don't call."

"Do you really believe that?"

"Yeah. I think so. Don't you? You're from New Orleans, after all. You told me once that your great-grandmother and grandfather held séances in their home."

"That's true."

"You also told me that both your grandmother and mother were extraordinarily psychic."

"That's true. And it's also true that I don't want a dead girl haunting me."

"Like on TV?"

"In any fashion!"

"So?"

"Okay. I'll call the police." Danni moved into the bedroom clutching the newspaper. She glanced down at the artist's rendering again, and drew her brows together. *No way is this Pete. There's some resemblance, but Pete doesn't have soulless eyes. The eyes of the man in the rendering have no life in them. It's as though his spirit had died. He does resemble Eddie. Maybe if I draw a pair of sunglasses on him.* She took the pen on the end table next to the bed and drew a pair of dark glasses on him. She paused and sucked in her breath. It was him. He'd been in her home, time and time again. Had he killed Tiffany?

She moved back into the room and glanced at Bobby.

"You're as pale as a sack of flour...not whole wheat either. What happened?"

"I didn't want to believe that it was either Pete or Eddie. It isn't Pete."

"Did you call the police?"

"No. I just figured it out. If it's Eddie, the person who called the description in left one important factor out. I've seen him only once without his sunglasses, but he has a big red scar on the bridge of his nose. The drawing doesn't."

"Maybe the artist made a mistake. He must have seen him from a distance."

"Maybe."

CHAPTER 23
MISTAKEN IDENTITY

Pete pulled into the small apartment near the inlet on North Longboat. Tiffany had quit-claimed it to him years ago. He smiled. She'd been fun, but he'd never loved her. She'd owed him money and he'd settled for the apartment. He'd like to see her again. Where was it she had told him that she was moving to? Ft. Myers? Maybe he'd look her up while he was there. She probably had a boyfriend or a husband, but what would that matter? It would be fun just to say "Hey."

Pete unlocked the door and began carrying his art supplies and fishing gear in. Last came his suitcases and the groceries he'd picked up. Once he'd put everything away, he popped open a beer and took it out to the screened-in porch that faced the inlet. When he finished the beer, he showered, fell into bed, and slept until nearly noon. He hadn't had much sleep last night. It wasn't easy to sleep scrunched down behind a steering wheel. If the SUV hadn't been so loaded with art supplies, he could have moved into the backseat. It had been a long drive to the apartment on Fisherman's Cove near Whitney Beach.

Setting up his easel and paints, he thought briefly about Danni. He shook his head. Women! He still wondered why she hadn't called. Maybe Vince wasn't dead. Maybe he'd hadn't reboarded the plane in Albuquerque. Maybe he'd left the airport, rented a car, and had an accident, or decided his life was so damn complicated he'd take a break and come back later. Or not. As for himself, he'd really fallen for Danni. All he could think about was her beautiful smile and her lovely sparkling green eyes. She'd messed him up so much, he felt like he needed to see a shrink. He shouldn't have gone to her house. That had been stupid.

After he'd set everything up and was just about to begin painting, he decided to make a ham and cheese sandwich. He moved to the fridge and pulled out all of the ingredients, and placed two slices of whole wheat bread on the plate. On one side of the bread he smeared a healthy amount of mayo, and on the other side…. Damn! He'd forgotten the mustard.

He grabbed his wallet and car keys, and headed out the front door to the store down the way, where he picked up the mustard and a carton of pecan butternut iced cream. When he went to the cash register, the elderly woman rang his meager purchases up, and then looked at him as though he had appeared straight off the set of a horror movie. He glanced down at his jeans. Maybe he'd forgotten to zip his pants up. Nope. That wasn't it.

"What's wrong?"

"Nothing." The cashier shook her head.

"You look like you've seen a ghost."

"Do you live around here?" the cashier asked.

"Why do you ask?" It was none of her business.

She shrugged her shoulders and placed his purchases in a sack. "Thank you, sir."

"Sure." Pete walked out of the store. When he glanced up, he saw that the cashier was on the phone. "Weird," he muttered to himself.

Starting the car, he drove back to the studio. Once there, he finished making the sandwich, popped another beer open, then carried his lunch out onto the screened-in back porch, which faced the inlet. He sat on the rattan sofa eating the sandwich and drinking the soda while he watched an old man fish near the mangroves.

For the rest of the afternoon and for the next three days he did nothing but paint and fish. Since he didn't watch TV or read the newspaper, he was oblivious to the world. The first painting that he did was of the inlet. The water was rough; palms leaned with the wind, a small boat, tied to a dock, rocked in the water, while rain fell in sheets. In actuality, it was a beautiful day with a few cumulous clouds passing overhead. The water was tranquil. An old man untied the boat, preparing to go for a ride.

When he stepped back to observe his work, it was clear to him that the scene had reflected his mood. Evidently, he was more than a just little disturbed. Pete knew why. He still hadn't heard from Danni and he'd checked for messages on his cell phone twice a day. He couldn't figure it out; he thought they'd become friends, but evidently, he'd been mistaken. Pete called her cell phone, but the number no longer belonged to her. His only alternative, other than driving back to Boca and walking into JVS Developer's office, was to call, which until now, he'd resolved not to do.

He moved into the kitchen where the cell phone was charging. Fully charged, he unplugged it and punched in JVS's telephone number.

"This is JVS Developers."

"May I speak with Danni Giardini, please?"

"I'm sorry, sir. Mrs. Giardini isn't here."

"Look, I'm a friend of hers and I need to reach her."

"She's not expected back for some time."

"Is there some way that I can reach her? It's an emergency."

"Yes, sir. Mrs. Giardini is currently working at our other

development on the other coast; in Sarasota."

"Where is your office located in Sarasota?"

"Just off of Clark Road and Honore. Do you need the telephone number?"

"Yes, thank you."

***

When he disconnected from the call, a corner of Pete's mouth lifted. He moved into the small bathroom, showered, shaved, and dressed in a crisp pair of white tennis shorts, white shirt, and tennis shoes. After he had splashed after shave lotion on, he headed out. On his way, he pulled into the Avenue of the Flowers on Longboat Key to pick up a newspaper and a bottle of water at the grocery store. When he came out of the store, he noticed a new hair salon in the shopping center. It couldn't hurt to get a haircut. He headed up the sidewalk and walked into the salon.

"May I help you, sir?"

"Yes. I'd like a cut. Is there anyone here who is available now?"

"I believe so. Let me check with Angela."

When she returned, she said, "She can do it in about ten minutes. Would that be all right?"

Pete nodded, turned, and sat down on one of the chairs. An elderly woman, her hair freshly styled, walked over and stopped to peer in his eyes.

"Ma'am, is there something I can do for you?"

"I thought you were him, but you're not."

"Who?"

"The killer, the one the police are looking for."

"It's not me." Pete shook his head. "I've never killed anyone."

"Ethyl," the receptionist said, "if you read the article again, the paper says that the police are interested in the man that is depicted in the rendering. It does not say that the person killed anyone."

"Doesn't matter. This isn't the man. I can tell by his eyes. You know, they say the eyes are the window to the soul. This man has the soul of a poet, or maybe an artist."

Pete smiled gently. "You must be psychic. I am an artist. Peter Langley Stevens."

"Oh my. I just love your paintings. I have one hanging in my living room. Are you here on location?"

He grinned. "In fact, I am."

"I'm Ethyl Simpson. I apologize for being so rude and staring at you. It's just that you do look a lot like the man in the rendering, but I can clearly see that you're not."

"No. I'm not."

"Please call me Ethyl. If I give you my address, will you ask your gallery to send me an invitation to your next opening? You do have a gallery that you're with here in Sarasota, don't you?"

"I'm sorry, I don't. Most of my paintings are with the Galleria del Sol in Palm Beach, as well as a new gallery in Boca Raton. However, I could ask the managers to send you a brochure."

"I'd love that."

"Mr. Langley, Angela is ready for you. Ethyl, if you will write your name and address down, I will see that Mr. Langley has it."

While Angela shampooed Pete's hair, he heard a familiar voice. A smile crept to his mouth.

***

"I called earlier and booked an appointment for a trim, wash, and blow dry about a half hour ago. My name is Danni Giardini."

"Jennie is ready for you, Ms. Giardini."

"Wonderful."

"Ms. Giardini?"

"Yes."

"I'm Jennie. Follow me please."

110

Escorted to Jennie's station, she set her handbag down on the counter, opened it, and pulled a photo from her wallet. "I just need a little trim. I usually wear it like this." Danni handed the photo to her.

"This will be easy."

Jennie placed a black waterproof cape around Danni and fastened it. Placing a towel around her neck, she escorted her to the shampoo bowls. Once she was in the chair, Pete rose and moved to Angela's station, which was in the front of the salon on the opposite side of Jennie's.

By the time Angela had finished, he wore a huge grin on his face. Paying the cashier and giving the operator a larger tip than normal, he moved to the sofa, picked up a magazine, and waited for Danni. Thirty minutes later, she walked up to the cashier. Not knowing what her reaction would be when she saw him, he rose, left the salon, and waited just outside the door.

"Danni," he said as she walked out of the salon.

"Pete! What are you doing here in Sarasota?"

"I have a studio here. I came over for a little solitude and to paint. What a coincidence running into you."

"Isn't it?"

"I've been trying for weeks to reach you. You know, you owe me lunch."

Danni felt the heat rising to her face. "I'm sorry. I understand that neither Sal nor his secretary called you to cancel our date."

"No. They didn't. I haven't been able to figure out what I did that angered you. Whatever it is, I apologize."

"You didn't do a thing, Pete. I feel terrible about this, but I'm so glad I ran into you today. Let me take you to lunch today and I'll explain."

Pete's spirits soared, and he grinned. "How could I refuse?"

"I know of a great restaurant on St. Armand's Circle. They

have outdoor seating as well as indoor. It's not too hot today, and they have a sidewalk piano bar."

"You're speaking of what was once Charlie's Crab, aren't you?" Pete asked.

She nodded. "I think it's the Fish and Fin now."

"I have my SUV if you would like to go in my car."

Danni smiled. "That would be great."

Once she'd explained what had happened and that she'd lost her cell with his phone number stored in it, Pete was relieved, but angry with Sal Catalano. He had no business interrupting their friendship. It was obvious to him that he was protecting his own interests in Danni. Hadn't Madison told him that Vince's partner had once dated Danni?

***

While they were waiting for menus at the Fish and Fin, Danni noticed that many of the customers were staring at Pete. Two women rose from their table and left.

Pete shook his head. "This happened to me at the salon today while I was waiting for my haircut. Did you by any chance see the artist's rendering and read the article about the creep that they are mistaking me for? I would sure like to give him a call."

"I saw it. I still have the article. I'll show it to you."

"Evidently you didn't think it was me or you wouldn't be here."

"First of all, I know that you wouldn't commit such a heinous crime. Secondly, even though you resemble the man that was shown in the paper, that person has eyes that are void of life. You don't."

Pete grinned. "So, do you think I have the eyes of an artist… or a poet? That's what a woman in the salon told me."

Danni laughed. "You have beautiful, sparkling, amber eyes, full of life, and stories to be told whether by words or on canvas."

"Well, thanks. I'm glad you feel that way. Don't be a stranger again."

"I won't. In fact, I'm going to introduce you to a friend of mine who is approaching our table. He's the son of our manager, Madeline Cummings, at JVS here in Sarasota. He may be able to help you out with your situation"

"What situation?"

"That of being a doppelganger to the wrong man."

"Well, Danni, I had heard you were in town with your adopted son, Bobby McMann," Officer Cummings said.

"Good afternoon, Joe. Please join us. I'd like you to meet a friend of mine. He is a wonderful artist and a financial wizard. Peter Langley, Officer Sal Cummings."

"Good afternoon, Officer." Pete stood, removed his sunglasses, and shook hands with the officer.

"Good afternoon, Mr. Langley. I wondered who you were when I first saw you. You know, or maybe you don't, that we've been looking for someone who closely resembles you."

Sitting back down, Pete nodded. "I wasn't aware of that until earlier this morning. I don't know who the artist was that did the rendering, but I sure would like to speak with him...or her. People have been scattering upon first sight of me."

"I'm sorry about that. We received a call from the person who gave the description earlier today. A correction will be in the newspaper tomorrow. It turns out the person we're looking for has a deep red scar across the bridge of his nose. He wears dark aviation glasses during the daytime...similar to yours, in fact."

"Oh man. I'd better pick up some new sunglasses."

Joe nodded. "It would be a good idea. In fact, you might think about buying a pair of big round ones with white frames."

Pete laughed. "Might as well. Danni mentioned this guy is of interest to the police. I still don't know what all of these people think I did."

Joe described the murder of a young woman in Ft. Myers and where her body was found.

"Before you go any further, Joe, I must tell you that until you mentioned the scar across the bridge of his nose, I wasn't sure if I had seen the person or not," Danni said. "I can tell you that not only have I seen him, but I know him."

"How do you know him?"

"He's my gardener. I hired him after Vince was killed,"

"Then you have his references."

"I have a form my employees fill out. But I was so upset after I'd heard that Vince had been killed that I didn't have Eddie complete it. We talked for a while and I wrote down some notes; where he'd worked before and a couple of references. I called them both, but could only reach one of them. I think her name was Tiffany. I don't know what her last name was though. After he began working for me, we became more like friends than employer/employee. He was a good worker and did a great job."

"Do you always become friendly with your employees?" Pete asked, with a concerned expression in his eyes.

"Most of the time, but not always. Eddie seemed to be so alone. He'd had a rough childhood. He had been passed around from one foster home to another. I felt badly for him."

Pete grinned. "Soft-hearted woman."

"That will get you in trouble. Does he still work for you?" Joe asked.

"He still takes care of the lawn, but since I moved out of the house, JVS pays him."

"Tell me more about this guy," Joe said. "Does he have any other scars other than the one on his nose? Any body piercings that you know of? Tattoos? You said he had foster parents. Where was he born? Where was he from? Did he have a girlfriend?"

"I noticed some small round scars, about the size of a pencil eraser, on his left forearm. As far as tattoos go, yes. He has a scorpion tattoo on his right forearm, and an eagle on his right shoulder. Uh...I know that because sometimes, when it's hot outside, he takes his shirt off when he's working."

"Hmm," Pete murmured. "It's not summer and it hasn't been very hot lately. I think he was showing off."

"Well, we've had a few warm days."

"What the hell?"

"What? A lot of workmen take their shirts off when it's hot."

"I wasn't referring to that, or to his showing off. A lot of men with good physiques would do that to impress you, Danni. What's this about the scorpion and the eagle?" Joe asked.

"He's either weird or he's familiar with the astrology symbols," Pete said.

"What do you mean?"

"If he's a Scorpio, his birthday could be between October 21 and November 21," Pete said. "The eagle and the scorpion are the symbols for those born under the sign of Scorpio."

Joe nodded. "Okay, so he's an astrology nut, too. Do you know anything about astrology, Danni?"

"A little. I have a friend who is an astrologer."

"Where does your friend live?"

"Sedona, Arizona."

"Of course," Joe said with a smirk.

"Pete, how much do you know about astrology?"

"Not much; just the birth signs."

"Danni, I may want the name and number of your friend who is an astrologer, depending upon how bizarre this case gets."

"That's no problem. His wife is a good friend of mine. They live part-time in Vero Beach, and the other half of the time in Sedona."

"Do you know where Eddie was born?"

"No. He said he'd recently moved from Ft. Myers to Pompano Beach."

Joe jotted the facts down in a small notebook, and then asked, "Girlfriend?"

Danni nodded. "He spent a lot of time going back and forth to visit a girl. She was, by the way, the only reference he gave that I was able to check out."

"Her name?" Joe asked.

"Tiffany. I don't remember her last name."

"Could it have been Owens?"

"I suppose so, but I can't say for sure."

"Jesus!" Joe's eyes widened.

"I know Tiffany Owens." Pete drew his brows together.

"How?" Joe asked, leaning over the table.

"She was a client of mine. Besides being an artist, I'm also a financial consultant. Actually, that's how I make my living."

"Are you independent or do you work for someone?"

"A couple of years ago I worked with a large investment company, but I'm on my own now."

Joe nodded. "Where did you get your degree?"

"From the University of Florida at Gainesville."

"That's where I went to school," Danni said. "Sal, Vince, and James went there, too."

"So did I," Joe said. "It's a popular school. Back to the subject of crime…Mom told me you were being stalked, Danni."

"How did she find out?"

"Sal Catalano, your partner, told her to watch out for you and Bobby. He saw the artist's rendering as well as the article, and believes that Eddie Haywood could be your stalker."

"Oh my God."

"He may also be Tiffany Owens's murderer."

"Murderer?"

Joe nodded. "She was beaten to death, stabbed in the heart, and dumped in a ditch near Ft. Myers."

"Oh God, no." Pete shook his head in denial. "She was a great girl. Beautiful, too. She wasn't only my client but a friend too. In fact, she once owned the studio that I have here."

"So, you bought it from her?"

"Not exactly. I loaned her some money, about seventy-five thousand, and she couldn't pay me back. Jokingly, I told her she could quit-claim her apartment to me since she wanted to move out of town."

Joe whistled. "And she did?"

"Yeah. The apartment wasn't worth more than that then."

"You got quite a deal," Joe said.

Pete nodded. "I'd like to help you find her killer, if I can."

"I think, maybe, you may both be of help to us in this case. How long are you going to be here, Danni?"

"I'm not sure. Sal sent me over here to check out the development in Sarasota and to make some improvements. But, I think he'd planned for Bobby and me to go to Austin in a week or two."

"Austin?" Joe asked. "Texas?"

"Yes."

"Why Austin?"

"Texas evidently has a better economy than Florida does. He believes both Midland and Austin may be ripe for a building project. He's sending us there to check it out."

"Pete, we're going to want you to stay in close contact until we solve this case. We need more help from you, too, Danni. I'll give Sal a call."

"I can stay around here for a while. But, I'd planned to go back to the other coast to check on my cousin in a couple of weeks. She's owns a bookstore in Tequesta, and is expecting her first child in a few months. She's not married, lives alone, and I'm concerned about her."

"What about the father? Isn't he around?"

"Unfortunately not," Pete said. "He was killed recently."

"It's complicated, Joe. I knew the father well. I can ask Sal to check on her."

"If you wouldn't mind," Pete said.

"Of course not."

"You two must know each other well. Family friends?"

Danni smirked. "You could say that, I suppose."

"Would you mind coming into the station after lunch, both of you? I think there are some questions that need to be answered in order to help us solve this case."

"Anything I can contribute to solving the case, I will," Danni affirmed.

"So will I."

"I'll need to pick up my car when I leave here, and call Bobby," Danni said. "I'm meeting him later this afternoon at the office."

"Which is where?" Joe asked.

"It's near Palmer Ranch off Clark Road."

"You will come by the police station first, won't you?"

"That's no problem, Officer. Danni's car is parked at the Avenue of The Flowers on Longboat. We'll pick her car up after lunch and she can follow me to the station."

Joe nodded. "That's fine. If you will excuse me, I'd better be getting back to work."

"It was nice meeting you." Pete stood to shake his hand. "I expect we'll see you at the station."

"Try to make it in an hour. I'd like to be there when you and Danni come in."

"We'll do that."

"Thanks, Joe. We'll see you soon."

Pete caught the waitress's eye and motioned her over. He sat back down. "Do you know what you would like for lunch, Danni?"

"Shrimp cocktail and iced tea, please."

"May I take your order, sir?"

"The same for me, and a basket of bread, please."

"Will that be all?"

"Unfortunately, we're in something of a rush."

"I'll have it right out, sir."

Pete sighed. "I think after all of that, I've pretty much lost my appetite."

"Me too."

***

After Danni started her car, she called Bobby on the way to the station and explained the situation. After that, she called Sal.

"This is not good news."

"What do you mean?" Danni asked. "It's good news for Pete. He's been cleared, but they will probably want him to remain here on this coast for further questioning."

"I wasn't speaking about Pete. Since he's obviously become a friend of yours, I want to meet him when I come to Sarasota. What I mean is, it isn't a good thing that Madison is pregnant and alone. I'll check in on her."

"Thanks. Pete will appreciate that."

"I'm worried about you, too. Eddie hasn't been found yet. Wasn't he last seen on that coast?"

"I think so. Officer Cummings mentioned that he might not want me to leave town just yet either."

"Huh! We'll see about that. You need to go straight to Austin," Sal said. "You're birthday's coming up soon, next week, in fact.

We could celebrate with Jazzy and do the clubs on Sixth Street."

"That would be fun!"

"So it's settled."

"Maybe. Joe mentioned that he would be getting in touch with you later today."

"Good. I'll speak with him about it. I'm sure it will be okay. After all, you had nothing to do with the murder."

"No. But the man we suspect is employed by me."

"Wrong, Beautiful. Officially, he's employed by JVS Builders. I know Eddie, too. I've cut him a few checks."

"So you would be able to identify him."

"Absolutely."

"I'm at the police station now, and I need to go in."

"Call me later this afternoon and let me know how it goes." Sal disconnected.

CHAPTER 24
ELIZABETH'S DEBUT

Sal rose from his chair, took his keys from out of the top drawer of his desk, and locked up the office. He drove straight home and packed a small bag. Headed north on I-95, he decided to check Madison's Bookstore before he continued on to Sarasota. On his way, he began thinking about how much time had passed since Vince had been dead or missing. It was now approaching the middle of May. If the doctor had been correct, Madison was expecting somewhere between mid-June to July. She'd looked damn pregnant the last time he'd seen her. *What if the baby's early? Step on it.*

Sal slammed down on the accelerator. *What the hell? Where did that thought come from?* He'd had a lot of hunches in his life, most of which had been advantageous to him. Being somewhat psychic, just as Danni was, he had no desire to ignore his gut feelings. He sped up and didn't stop once for gas or a soda. All lights had been green from the time he'd felt the urgent prodding.

Sal drove into the strip mall in Tequesta and pulled into a parking spot in front of Madison's Bookstore. He opened the door of the Porsche, stepped out of the car, and headed into the store. Madison was on her hands and knees on the floor with her rear up in the air in a pool of tainted water. At a closer glance, he saw her cell phone lying two to three feet away from her. Evidently she'd been crawling, making her way to her cell phone to call for help.

He rushed to her.

"Call 911," Madison said in a weak voice. "Hurry."

Sal took his cell phone in hand and punched in 911.

"My water broke," Madison said.

"It's too early, isn't it?"

"Uh-huh." Tears ran down Madison's cheeks." But, the baby's coming now."

Sal relayed the information to the 911 operator.

"Stay with her until someone arrives."

"What do I do? What if she has the baby before the EMT's arrive?" Beads of perspiration broke out on his forehead.

"Stay on the line with me until they get there."

Seconds later, a woman walked in the door. "What's wrong?" she asked.

"Madison.... The EMT's will be here soon."

"I'm Jeannie, the assistant manager, mid-wife, as well as Madison's best friend. What happened?"

"She says her water broke. The baby's coming. I called 911. I have the operator on the line just in case the baby comes first."

"It's okay. I know what to do. You can hang up now."

"Not a good idea. I'll hang up when the EMT's arrive."

Jeannie walked over and kneeled down next to Madison. "It's okay. We're here with you, and an ambulance is on its way. You'll be at the hospital in nothing flat."

Madison groaned.

Jeannie glanced up at Sal. "I don't think I've met you. Are you a customer?"

"Huh? No. I'm Sal Catalano. Er…one of Vince's partners. I just stopped by to see how she's doing."

"Just out of the blue?"

"Yeah. I was actually on my way over to the other coast."

The door to the bookstore opened; EMT's rushed in and went straight to Madison. "We've got to get her to the hospital. She's in labor," Jeannie told them.

"Are you the father?" they asked.

"No. Just a friend."

"Better contact the father."

"He's deceased."

"You're not serious," Jeannie said. "Please tell me that's not true."

"I am serious, and I wish it weren't true."

"Oh my God!" Jeannie glanced at the driver of the ambulance. "Please, let me ride with you. I'm her best friend."

"Come along with us."

"I'll put the closed sign on the door and lock up."

Jeannie nodded. "Okay. Just turn the lock when you leave, Sal."

"Wait! Here's my card. Call me on my cell phone and let me know how things are going. I'll pass the news on to Pete."

"Where is he?"

"On the other coast."

"Better tell him to come back. Madison's going to need him."

"I'm not sure he's going to be able to do that. It's a long story, but I'll see what I can do," Sal said. "Can you stay with her for a couple of weeks until he gets back?"

"I plan to. Right now, she has no one else."

"Where's her mother?"

"Her mother's deceased. She died of breast cancer about five years ago. She has no sisters or brothers."

"I'm sorry to hear that. What about her dad?"

"He's in China, working on a project of some kind."

"So, she's all alone until he returns to the States?"

"Except for Pete, I'm afraid so. I've gotta' go now. They'll leave without me," Jeannie said, running for the emergency vehicle.

***

Sal drove up Interstate 95 wishing that he could have had a cold beer after he'd left the bookstore. He'd never in his adult life taken a drink before he got behind the wheel. No way was he going to take a chance on hurting anyone or ending up in jail with a DUI now. When he reached Ft. Pierce, he turned west on Highway 72. Stopping at a gas station in Okeechobee, he filled up and picked up a newspaper. A couple of hours down the road, he stopped at a small country restaurant in Arcadia for a hamburger. While he was waiting, he opened the paper and began to read. He drew his brows together. Setting the paper down, he called Danni.

"Sal!"

"Where are you, and are you going to be able to leave town for Austin soon?" Sal asked.

"Yes. But Pete is going to need to stay here."

"Why?"

"Pete knew the murder victim. The police believe that he may be able to help them find the killer."

"Huh." He started to tell her about Madison, but decided to wait until he met her at the office in Sarasota.

"Do you have Pete's number?"

"Yes. Hold on while I pull into this car wash."

***

Danni turned and pulled the car up to the front, counting her blessings that there wasn't a line today. "Just a basic car wash, citrus scent." Taking her ticket, she stepped out of the car and walked over to the entrance of the car wash, which faced

124

Highway 41. Before she went inside, she paused to shuffle through her purse. "Okay Sal. I found it," she said, giving him Pete's cell number.

"I need to give him a call. Be careful."

Chapter 25
A Narrow Escape

The corners of Eddie's mouth turned up and his eyes widened. He pulled over into the left-hand lane and did a U-turn. Was that Danni he'd seen at the car wash? He could swear it was. He drove by slowly. Yep. There she was, stepping out from the office of the car wash. He drove around the block a couple of times, then parked in the lot of the pharmacy next door.

***

Danni drew her brows together. The same truck had driven by several times. He pulled into the business next to the car wash and parked. Ordinarily she wouldn't have noticed, but with everyone warning her to be careful, she was on "red alert." The truck looked like Eddie's.

The cell phone jingled. "Hey, Beautiful. Where are you now?"

"I'm waiting for my car at the car wash on Highway 41 near Stickney Point road. Oh! It's ready now. A truck that resembled Eddie's drove by a couple of times, then parked in the lot at Walgreen's next door. The driver's still sitting in the truck. Do you think it's Eddie?"

"Could be. Don't go to the office. When you leave, go right on 41, do a U turn, and drive to the light at the corner of Clark Road. Take a left and turn into the fire station. It will be on your right."

"All right."

"Tell them what you just told me. I'll meet you there."

"Thanks."

***

"Hey."

"Pete. Sal Catalano here, Danni's partner. We haven't met yet, but I need your help. I'm on my way into Sarasota. Danni may be in trouble. Are you anywhere near Highway 41 and Clark Road?"

"I'm in a shopping center near Clark and Highway 41."

"Good enough. Can you go to the fire station on Clark Road just off Highway 41? I think Eddie's tailing her in a white F250 pick up. I told her to go to the station and wait for me. She should be there now. I'm on my way in from Arcadia."

"I'm on my way." Pete moved the shopping cart full of art supplies to the side. "Be back later to pay for these," he hollered to the cashier on his way out of the door. He ran to his car, clicked open the door, climbed into the SUV, and sped out of the center.

***

Danni drove to the station, turned the ignition off, and watched while the pickup slowed down. The driver turned left at the corner. He was going around the block. She got out of the car, ran into the station, and spoke to the captain. "My partner's going to meet me here. I think I'm being followed."

"You did the right thing, miss. Is that your partner pulling up now?"

She turned. "It's a friend. Pete! How did you know I was here?"

"Sal called me. He'll be here soon. What's going on?"

She introduced him to the captain and explained.

"From now on," Pete said, "I don't think you should be out

alone. Between me, Sal, and Bobby, one of us can be with you."

***

Sal pulled in, jumped out of the car, and went straight to where Danni and Pete were standing.

"Did you get a look at the driver?"

"It could have been Eddie," Danni said. "I can't say for sure, but it looked like his truck."

"It looked like the same truck that I saw leaving the picnic area outside of Clewiston," Pete said. "But then, old white Ford 250's are common around Florida."

"Before this interruption, Danni and I were going to meet at JVS's models near Clark and Honore. Just in case this guy's still hanging around, why don't you leave your car parked here, Danni? You can ride with me to the models. Pete, if you have time, I'd like to talk with you about your cousin, Madison. Can you meet us there?"

"Sure."

"Pete's never been to the models. I'll go with him and we'll meet you at the sales office."

"Okay." Sal moved to speak with the captain.

Fifteen minutes later, both cars arrived in front of the sales office. "No one's here," Danni said. "I wonder where the salesperson is?"

"I don't know, but it's no wonder you're not selling homes," Pete replied.

When they entered the office, she immediately spotted another problem. It was messy. A half a donut and crumbs lay on a napkin near the computer.

"Maybe you need another salesperson and a cleanup crew here, Sal."

"I'll say. Let's go into the conference room. After we complete our business, we'll view the models. Pete, would you like a beer?

Danni? A glass of wine?"

"A beer would be great."

"I'd love a glass of chardonnay, if there is any. You know beer gives me a headache."

"There's only white zinfandel."

"That'll be fine."

Sal entered the conference room with a tray full of assorted appetizers and drinks. He wanted to speak to Pete about Madison, but not until he'd finished his beer. He figured if Pete was anything like he was, he'd want to head straight out across the coast to see Madison and maybe, by now, the baby.

"First of all, Pete, I need to apologize to you. Since Vince's death, I've been guarding Danni like a hawk. I knew she was being stalked and in danger, especially after the event with the intruder."

"What happened?" Pete asked, setting his beer down on the table.

After Danni had explained, Sal said, "I moved her things out of her house right away, and after Danni agreed, we put it up for sale. The day she was to have lunch with you, she wanted to call you and explain why she couldn't keep the date. But I wanted her to leave the area and promised her that my secretary would contact you. She didn't come in that day, and I'm sorry to say that I forgot all about it."

Pete ran his fingers through his curly, sandy blond hair. "Thanks for the apology. I agonized for weeks over that."

Danni set her mouth. She glanced up at Sal. "You shouldn't have interfered. That never should have happened."

"No. I'm sorry. It shouldn't have. I made a bad judgment call, but I was just so worried about you, Danni."

"Apology accepted," she said.

"Thank you, both of you. Another beer, Pete? I've something

else to tell you."

"Think I'll need it?"

"Yeah."

"Is this about you, Danni?"

"No. I don't know what it's about. Think I need a refill?"

"Maybe."

Pete removed the bottle of wine from the chiller and refilled her glass.

Sal handed the beer to Pete and said, "I stopped by to see Madison at the bookstore on my way over this afternoon."

"How is she?"

"She's in the hospital. When I arrived, her water had just broken and she was in labor. I called 911 just about the time her friend Jeannie walked in. She's with her now, and will stay as long as Madison needs her."

"Damn!" Pete jumped up from the chair. "I need to get over there."

Sal slapped his hand down on the table a couple of times and laughed. "I thought that would be your reaction. It would have been mine. Don't worry. Madison's in good hands. I've called my doctor and he will be looking in on her as well as the baby. He's going to call me later. Both he and his wife are going up to see them tomorrow morning. They're friends of mine and of Danni's. In fact, they were close friends of Vince's, and can't wait to see the baby."

"That must have been quite an ordeal for you, Sal." Glancing over to Pete, Danni explained. "Sal's still a bachelor. He's never been married or around children, much less women in labor."

Pete leaned back in his chair and laughed. "I'm not sure I could have handled that myself. I was wondering how I was going to help Madison through childbirth. Frankly, I'm glad it was Jeannie and not me."

"Well, shall we begin touring the properties? Pete, if you don't want to come with us, you don't need to."

Danni glanced at Pete. "I'd really like you to come with us, if you have time. Some of these models could use a mural. You might be interested."

"I might. That is, if Madison doesn't need me right away. Officer Cummings has told me that he needs me here, in Sarasota and Manatee counties, for a while. I don't know why. I'm not sure what sort of information he believes I can provide him with."

"No hurry. Let's lock up the office, tour the properties, and move on to the club for dinner."

***

After a long dinner, Pete felt as though he'd been accepted as one of their closest friends. He'd sure like to be a lot more than a friend to Danni, but considering that she'd recently lost her husband and discovered that he'd betrayed her, it might take time for her to recover from both the loss and the betrayal. Though his blood ran hot and he could barely keep his hands off her, he'd force himself to be patient and to prove to her that he was a good man. He would never have cheated on her.

While they were having dessert, Sal's cell phone rang.

"Madison! I didn't expect you! Yes, Pete's here, but before I hand the phone over to him, tell me how you and the baby are." Sal grinned and glanced at Pete. "Madison has a beautiful new baby girl, a month early, but she weighs nearly six pounds. She wants to name her Elizabeth Victoria after her mother." He handed Pete the cell phone.

"That's a beautiful name, for a beautiful little girl, and she will be christened after a wonderful woman. Are you all right?" Pete glanced at Sal, covered the mouthpiece, and said, "She says of course she's all right."

Danni laughed and shook her head. "I doubt I would be."

"Call me tomorrow. Oh! And don't forget to call your dad." Pete clicked off the cell phone.

"Well, a toast to Elizabeth Victoria Langley."

"That should be Elizabeth Victoria Langley-Giardini." The edges of Danni's lips curved up. "I wonder if there is a way that can be made right. I'm sure Vince would have liked the child to have his name. If he hadn't been killed, I'd have insisted on a divorce. They would have been married by now."

"What if he's still alive?" Sal asked, drawing his thick black brows together.

"Hmm. Right now, he's married to me. I need to take care of that in the unlikely event that Vince survived the crash and is in a hospital somewhere. I'm going to file for a Dissolution of Marriage before I leave for Texas."

"I think that's a good idea. For one, it will give you closure on your marriage. Since only a watch that we believe to have been Vince's was found, but not his body, we don't know for certain whether he's dead or alive. I think that you will need to post a notice in the newspaper when you file. I've had my doubts all along that Vince was killed. I still do. I don't think he would have reboarded the plane in Albuquerque. For that reason, I haven't filed for his life insurance or canceled his health insurance. I've also left his account with JVS open, just in case he's still alive and needs the money."

Danni nodded. "You must know something I don't. I'll call my attorney tomorrow."

Pete smiled and considered Danni in a new light. She was definitely on her way to becoming a single woman, and would legally be available to marry again if she wished to. Maybe, in time, he would have a chance with her. She was definitely worth waiting for.

***

Eddie pulled out of the development minutes after Sal, Danni, and Pete left. Staying a few cars behind them, he followed Danni and Pete to Longboat Key and watched as they turned into the club. Thinking Pete was going to drop her off, he waited. After thirty-five minutes had passed and Pete still hadn't come out, he left. After all, he was damn sure that it was Sal, not Pete that was in his way. He didn't need to follow him. Eddie left and drove on up to Bradenton, thinking that he had obtained all of the information he needed. It was only a matter of time before he had Danni just where he wanted her.

In the meantime, he had big plans for Sal. *Danni and I are friends again. All I need to do is get Sal out of the way. It's been him all along. In time, Danni and I could be more than friends. I'll wait for a year, the normal time for grieving. But, it's clear that Sal is making a move on her. I know exactly how to get even with him.* He barked out a shrill laugh. *Man, is Sal going to be pissed. Talk about fun!*

CHAPTER 26
UP IN FLAMES

Sal did his best to make airline reservations to Austin for Danni and Bobby for the next day, but he wasn't able to book either of them that week or the next. As long as Eddie didn't know Danni was still in Sarasota and that they had a branch of JVS here, he supposed she would be safe working at the models. It would also give the detectives more time to ask questions.

***

Danni rose early, dressed in her bathing suit, and prepared to go for an early beach walk and maybe a swim. Both Sal and Bobby were still sleeping. Slipping on a colorful shirt and a pair of capris, she stepped into a pair of slides. Grabbing her beach bag, she tossed in a brush, lipstick, a fashion magazine, and tanning lotion. Hitching it over her shoulder, she took her slim wallet from the table and tucked it as well as her car keys into her jeans. Placing a straw hat on her head, she picked up the key to the room, tossed it in the beach bag, and left, deciding at the last minute to drive to the restaurant up the road near downtown Bradenton Beach for breakfast. She was hungry and wanted more than just a sweet roll. Approaching the security gate, she was amazed to find it open with a sign that read Out of Order. There was not a guard on duty either. She suspected that later in

134

the day there would be a security guard at the entrance if the gate wasn't repaired by the time she returned. They would have been just as well off staying in one of the model homes.

***

Sitting in a booth near the middle of the restaurant, Danni skimmed over the front page of the Bradenton Herald. Taking a sip of hot coffee, she heard a familiar masculine voice.

"Hey! What's my gorgeous boss up to?"

Danni's heart went to her throat. She set the coffee down, and then folded the paper.

"Eddie!"

"Didn't expect to see me here, did you?"

She swallowed, and then laughed. "What are you doing in Bradenton? I thought you were working in Highland Beach today."

"I needed a vacation. Someone else is filling in for me. We need to catch up."

Sweet Jesus! Why hadn't she waited for Sal or Bobby this morning? Or called Pete to meet her?

***

"Mind if I sit down, maybe order some eggs and bacon?"

"Of course not. I'll buy."

This is more like it. Maybe she isn't sleeping with Sal. Maybe I still have a chance with her. She's not going anywhere. From now on, she's staying with me.

"What a deal! Man, am I hungry. I missed dinner. I haven't had a bite to eat since noon yesterday."

"Order whatever you want, steak and eggs with hash browns, or maybe eggs Benedict."

"That's my girl."

I'm not your girl, she wanted to correct him, but bit her tongue instead.

Halfway through breakfast, the hair at the nape of Danni's neck began to rise. Her throat went dry. The few times that she'd felt like that during her life was just before something really bad was about to happen. A sense of urgency warned her to leave before it was too late.

"If you will excuse me for a moment, I need to visit the ladies' room."

He stopped eating, set his fork down, and paused. "You do intend to come back, don't you?" The tone of his voice was hard.

"Sure, Eddie. Is there some reason you think that I wouldn't?"

He was silent for a minute, his jaw clenched. His soulless eyes flashed. "I don't know. You didn't tell me why you put your house up for sale and moved out without telling me. Friends don't do that."

Oh boy! He's pissed off.

"I'm sorry about that. I was having a multitude of problems, but we can talk about it later. Would you watch my beach bag for me while I go to the ladies' room?"

His shoulders relaxed. He picked up his fork and stabbed a piece of steak. "Sure. You can leave your bag here. I'll watch it." Eddie turned his attention back to his food.

"Okay. Thanks."

Once inside the ladies' room, she locked the door and surveyed her surroundings. Ugh! It was just the sort of public restroom that she hated. The restaurant was old and hadn't been remodeled. Neither had the bathroom. She held her breath. It was dirty and smelled. It contained a rusty old sink, a toilet that probably hadn't been flushed for a week, and a wastebasket that was overflowing with unmentionables.

Above the toilet was a small window, large enough for a petite woman her size to crawl out of. It was raised about a half inch, to allow for fresh air. She tore off a long strip of toilet paper and put the lid to the toilet down so that she could stand on it. Raising the window until it was wide open, she pushed the screen out. It wasn't far to the ground; maybe four feet. She could make it. She had to.

She straddled the window frame. Bringing her other leg up and over until she was sitting on the windowsill, she jumped. Landing on the ground, she glanced around and ran as fast as she could toward her car. Taking the keys from her pocket, she clicked the fob to open the door. Praying to God Eddie hadn't looked out of the window next to the booth that they had been sitting in, she opened the car door, slid in, locked the doors, and tore out of the lot, spraying gravel. She headed toward the club and prayed that Sal or Bobby would be there to open the door to the suite for her.

***

Sal rose and padded out to the kitchen to make coffee. He waited until it perked, poured a cup, and moved out onto the veranda, where he expected to see Danni. When she wasn't there, he went back in and knocked on the door to the bedroom she'd chosen to sleep in.

"Danni?"

There was no answer.

He opened the door and peeked in. She wasn't in bed. He moved to the bathroom. The door was open…she wasn't there either. A damp bath towel lay on the floor. Cosmetics were scattered over the counter. Her bathing suit was no longer hanging on the door hook. He reasoned she'd either gone to the beach or for a swim. Damn! He'd told her not to go anywhere alone.

He ran his hands through his hair, went back into his room, and pulled on his swim trunks and a shirt. Grabbing his room key, he left for the pool. She wasn't there. Suspecting she might have done something foolish, he checked to see if her car was parked in its proper space. It wasn't. He cursed and turned to walk back to the suite.

A horn blared behind him, and he turned to see Danni speeding into the lot, nearly running over him.

He stopped and waited till the car door opened and Danni jumped out.

"Thank God you're still here. Oh my God! I don't have the key to the room. I just remembered! It's in the beach bag that I left back in the restaurant. It's with Eddie! With Eddie! For God's sake, he has the key to our room now and knows where we're staying! Sweet Jesus! Why didn't I listen to you and Pete?"

"What's going on? Where have you been? Why did you see Eddie?"

"I left to have breakfast at a restaurant in Bradenton Beach. He came in and saw me."

"Damn! Why did you do that? I told you not to go anywhere without us."

"You were both sleeping. I didn't think it would make any difference. I certainly didn't expect Eddie to show up; not in Bradenton. Can we stop talking about this now? I know Eddie will come after me. He's going to be sooo mad! I lied to him to get away."

"If only Tiffany had done that, she might still be alive."

"She might be."

"You made a bad decision by going without us. But thank God you sensed that you were in danger and escaped."

She nodded. "He'll come after me."

"I don't think the guards will allow him to pass through the gate."

"The gate's broken, and no one's there."

"All right, the first order of the day is to have a new key made or move to a new suite."

"No. No, Sal. It won't matter if we are in a different suite. Eddie will find us. He's a nice-looking guy. He has a lot of charisma. Women love him, at least at first. He'll find out where we are. The desk clerk or even the maids will tell him."

"Calm down. I'm not going to let him come close to you. Tell me exactly what happened and what he said at breakfast."

***

She told him briefly what happened as they walked to the hotel lobby. As she did, she realized that it shouldn't have seemed so threatening up until the point that Eddie had said, "Friends don't do that." But it had been threatening and she'd known it. From the beginning she'd felt an ominous overtone to his presence, maybe because he was suspected to be the murderer of Tiffany Owens. She'd known that he was repressing his anger. Maybe it was her sixth sense, but she felt as though he'd intended to kidnap her. Sal was going to think she was ridiculous for climbing out of the window and running. She glanced over to him. "You think I'm crazy, don't you?"

"For going out alone? Yes. From what you're telling me, his words and actions in the restaurant wouldn't have alarmed a person who knew nothing about him. But you do. It's my bet that he had something up his sleeve. I'm sure he never intended to let you go. What alarmed you?"

"Maybe because he matches the artist's rendering. Or maybe because he was angry that I'd placed the house on the market and moved out without telling him. I had a really strong urge to run."

"Like a hunch. That's more like it."

"Do you think he would have kidnapped me? And later, killed me?"

Sal sighed. "Yes. I think he would have kidnapped you. As

far as killing you, probably not right away. But eventually, yes I think so. Remember, you wouldn't have been the first."

The color drained from Danni's face. "That's right. I wouldn't have been. It's a good thing I thought to put my car keys, my driver's license, and money in my jeans when I dressed this morning. I'd have been out of luck if I'd tossed them in the beach bag."

Sal frowned. "Maybe we should check out."

"Now?"

"Just as soon as we're packed. We'll stay at one of the models until we can find a flight out of Tampa. I'll call Joe and tell him what's happened and where we are going after we leave."

***

Twenty-five minutes later, they were all packed and ready to go when an explosion rocked the building. Sal ran to the window that faced the far parking lot.

"Damnation!"

"What happened?"

"Did a bomb explode?" Bobby asked, running to the window.

"My Porsche."

"It's going up in flames," Bobby yelled.

"Eddie did it. I know he did. He's blaming you, Sal. He believes you're keeping me away from him. He wants to hurt you and everything you hold dear."

"Danni, call Pete. Warn him. He may be next. You've been seen with him, too."

"Good idea."

"It sounds like Eddie has a mental disorder like I studied in psychology class last semester," Bobby said. "It's called a borderline personality disorder, or a BPD. Marsha Linehan, one of the world's leading experts on the disorder, describes it as the psychological equivalent of third-degree burn patients."

140

"Why?"

"They have no emotional skin. The slightest touch or movement can create immense suffering for those that suffer from the disorder."

"Oh, my God."

"No kidding. Above and beyond schizophrenics, patients with multiple personality disorders, the borderlines are the patients that psychologists fear most. About seventy-five percent hurt themselves."

Danni drew her narrow brows together. "Like putting cigarettes out on their arms? I remember seeing small round scars on Eddie's arms."

"Perfect example. These people have no internal governor, but they are capable of deep love and enormous rage simultaneously. They are tremendously connected to people close to them, and terrified of losing them," Bobby explained. "Believe it or not, they attack the very people they love because they fear they will abandon them."

"Can this disorder be treated with medication or therapy?" She wondered if a BPD, like schizophrenia or a bio-polar disorder, could be treated so that the patient could lead a normal life and live among others without endangering them.

Bobby shook his head. "Most therapists don't know how to treat patients afflicted with a BPD. Worse yet, the diagnosis of the condition is happening more frequently now. In 2008, a study of nearly thirty-five thousand adults in the *Journal of Clinical Psychiatry* found that 5.9%, or about eighteen million, Americans have been given a borderline personality diagnosis. At one time it was believed the disorder affected more women, but the latest research tells us that gender makes no difference. Adults in their twenties are at the highest risk."

"If you suspect that someone close to you has a BPD, how

should you treat them?" Danni asked with a worried expression on her face.

"Stay away from them when they are faced with an event that depresses or angers them. They will react by either becoming inconsolable or enraged."

"In other words, they are flat-out dangerous. You don't want to anger them, stress them out, or lead them on in any way."

"That's about it," Bobby said. "Do you remember the movie *Fatal Attraction*, starring Michael Douglas and Glenn Close, the sexy blonde that was a psycho?"

Danni nodded. "That movie frightened me to death."

"Just as it was meant to. The character that Glenn Close played suffered from a borderline personality disorder."

"Eddie fits the description."

"He's dangerous. Stay away from him, Aunt Danni."

"How are we going to leave from here without him seeing us? He's probably watching the fire."

Sal drew his heavy black brows together. "Don't you think, if he set the explosion, he'd be miles away from here?"

"No way." Bobby shook his head. "I think he'd be watching your Porsche burn and enjoying the sight."

"I think he's waiting for you and Bobby to leave. He's waiting to catch me alone again. He's going to kill me for running out on him. He will consider it a betrayal; an abandonment."

"He'll abduct you the first chance he gets. But, it's Sal, maybe even Pete, he wants to kill."

"They didn't leave him at the restaurant."

"No. But, he doesn't want to believe that you abandoned him. He'll tell himself that you wouldn't have left him unless someone had urged you to; someone like Sal."

Police sirens and fire engines sounded in the distance. Sal's cell phone rang.

"Yes, I know that my car has been destroyed. Where was security? Have you any idea of who did it? Let us know what you find out. Please send a security guard to the room. We've decided to check out and we need someone to escort us to our rental car. We have reason to believe that Ms. Giardini and possibly myself are in grave danger." Sal clicked off, called Pete, and quickly related the story from Danni's incident to his Porsche blowing up. He then called Officer Joe Cummings. "Hey, if you possibly can, please allow Pete to return to the other coast to be with his cousin, Madison, and her newborn child."

Officer Cummings refused to allow Pete to return to Tequesta, Florida, until after he'd investigated the murder case of Tiffany Owens further. Pete, he thought, might still be able to furnish more information in regard to Tiffany's habits and lifestyle.

"I'm sorry you feel that way, Officer. I believe Eddie's the killer and Pete is in danger. We suspect Eddie believes that both Pete and I are keeping Danni from him. My partner, Bobby McMann, is studying psychology at the university, and believes that Eddie suffers from a borderline personality disorder. Check with the psychologist there and you may decide to let Pete go."

CHAPTER 27
EDDIE'S THRILLS

Eddie's eyes glowed with excitement. He grinned wickedly as he watched the fire consume the black Porsche. Sal had just lost one of his most prized possessions. He deserved it. After all, it was he who moved Danni out of her home and placed it on the real estate sales market. It was he who had sent the movers to pick up her belongings. She wouldn't have done it on her own.

If she were having problems with the house, she would have discussed it with Eddie. They were friends. The proof that Sal had forced her into it was clear. He'd taken her away from him; disconnected her telephone. He couldn't and wouldn't blame sweet Danni for something she hadn't done.

Sal must have been outside of the restaurant motioning to Danni to come out, to leave him sitting there alone and stuck with the bill. Danni liked him; trusted him. She had proven that to him when she'd left her beach bag with him. He smiled to himself. She'd even left him the key to her room. She hadn't been brazen about it; hadn't been obvious. But, she'd left the key in the beach bag for him to find. He warmed to think of how he'd take her in his arms once her period of mourning was over. A vision of Danni lying naked beside him with drops of perspiration on her neck, décolleté, and breasts left him breathless and in need.

Once she was his, he'd never allow her out of his sight. She'd never leave him for a moment; not until she took her last breath.

For now, it was time to leave; to disappear. He climbed back into his pickup truck and headed for the glades. By sundown, he was back in his wood and glass home that had been built on stilts near Everglades City. He'd never told anyone about it except his close buddies and Tiffany. He'd brought her here for a weekend once, but that was before she'd double crossed him.

Crazy Lou, one of his foster brothers from Miami, had willed the home and land to him just before he'd been shot up in a drug war. He'd offered him a chance to get in on a lot of profitable drug deals, but he'd never joined Lou in his endeavors. He'd never done drugs, nor had he sold them. He didn't like the thought of kids, some not even teenagers, getting hooked on them. If Lou had felt the same, he'd probably still be alive. Still, a man with a history of arrests like Lou didn't have many choices as far as making an honest living. He'd had to do whatever he could.

Eddie had never made a judgment call on Crazy Lou for his choices. He'd had a big heart and had always helped him out. Not many had, except for a couple of women, like Tiffany, who had eventually betrayed him. He'd felt badly about the lesson he'd had to teach each of them. But, with the exception of Tiffany, he'd given the others a sunset burial in remembrance of the good times they'd shared. He was convinced that it was more than most men would have given them.

He unlocked the door to the house, set his bag down, and popped a beer open. Taking it out onto his lush patio, he sat down in a rattan settee he'd bought at a garage sale in Marco Island. Propping up his feet on a glass top coffee table, he leaned back, closed his eyes, and visualized just how he would kidnap Danni. He hadn't wanted to take her by force, but that was going to be the only way now. He didn't need to do it himself. He knew more than just a couple of guys who would do it for a six-pack or an ounce or two of the best blow money could buy.

CHAPTER 28
SAL'S DEPARTURE

They'd been staying in the largest model for over a week. So far, there had been no sign of Eddie. The police had not been able to locate him on either coast. The insurance company had taken care of Sal's claim, and a brand new Carrera was being delivered next week to the address Sal had chosen.

"Hey, beautiful, I'll be leaving for Boca this afternoon. I think you will be safe here. I don't think Eddie will be back in this county for a long time. There are posters of him everywhere. Just stay close to Pete and Bobby."

Danni nodded. "I will. When will you be back?"

"In a week or so. What do you have planned this afternoon?"

"I have an appointment with the hairstylist."

"That sounds safe, but take your cell phone with you, and be sure to tell Pete or Bobby where you are going."

"You're going to see Madison, aren't you?" Sal nodded. "I'll tell Pete. Be sure to give us a call later. Maybe call from Madison's. He'll want to talk to her."

Sal grinned. "You surprise me. Is it possible that you've forgiven Madison?"

She shrugged her shoulders. "There's nothing to forgive Madison for. She didn't do anything wrong."

"I'm glad you see it that way."

"How could I see it any other way?"

"Some women would."

"But I'm not some women."

"No. You're unique."

"Don't misunderstand me. If Madison had known Vince was married when she had the affair with him, I would not be so forgiving."

"I'm sure not. But that wasn't the case. As good of friends as you and Pete are, I expect you will be meeting her soon."

Danni blanched. Could she really handle meeting Madison, Vince's mistress, and their child? It wasn't going to be easy. Especially since she had wanted to have children with Vince herself. They say there are no victims, just volunteers. But wasn't she the victim of a married man's error?" Maybe it just depended upon how she looked at it. Their child was related to Pete. He was going to love the baby, and though he didn't know it yet, she loved him. Maybe she could view this little tiny person in a new and wonderful light.

CHAPTER 29
FLORAL DELIVERY

It was time, Eddie decided, to let Danni know that he hadn't lost interest in her. He'd followed them after the fire and knew exactly the model home that they were staying in. He planned to surprise her one morning when she least expected it. He drove into town to the local florist and arranged to have a dozen red roses sent to Danni, to be delivered to the JVS Sales office in Sarasota.

***

Pete arrived at the sales office around ten a.m., thinking it would just be a normal boring day at JVS Sales. In his opinion, it would save them money if they just rented the models and closed the operation down. No one was buying and few were looking. Nearing June, it would be hurricane season soon.

Much to his surprise, by three p.m. he'd sold not one, but two homes. Pleased, he decided to close early. Ready to lock up, he was stopped by a delivery man.

"You must have the wrong place."

"I don't think so. This is the JVS Sales Office, isn't it?"

"Yes."

"That's exactly where I'm to leave these flowers."

Pete drew his brows together. "Who are they for?"

149

"Danni Giardini."

Remembering that her birthday was coming up, he didn't ask the florist who they were from. "Okay. Come in. Set them on the end of the bar, please."

When the deliveryman left, Pete pulled out the card and read it.

To Danni,
My gorgeous boss
I haven't forgotten about you.
See you soon,
Eddie

Pete moved to the phone, picked it up, and punched in Officer Cummings' number.

"Officer Cummings. Pete here. I just received a dozen red roses for Danni. They were from Eddie. There's a personal note here with them."

"I'd like to see the note. What was the name of the florist that sent them?"

"I don't know. Maybe the delivery was arranged through an Internet florist."

"Still, you would think there would be a name of a florist on the card."

"Maybe Eddie bought the card and asked the florist to enclose it."

"The name of the florist should have been on the delivery truck. Where's Danni now?"

"At the hair salon."

"Keep a close eye on her."

"I will."

"You didn't by any chance see the delivery truck?"

"No. I was working here, in the sales office."

"There are people living in some of the units there, aren't there?"

"Yes, but I'm not sure which units are occupied. I'm sure there's some information around here about that. I'll ask Danni where it is when she comes in."

"I'll check around. Maybe someone saw the delivery truck," Officer Cummings said.

CHAPTER 30
ABDUCTED!

Eddie took a slug of beer and laughed. *Gotta do this myself, but it will be fun. Can't take a chance with the dirt bags I know. I'll surprise her tomorrow morning when she leaves for her morning beach walk. She won't know it's me or where I'm taking her. Ralph and Henry, both pits, will be guarding the front and back doors so she can't leave once she's here. The only safe way out is through the carport, but she won't know that. Jake, my chow, and the orneriest of the dogs, will be on a short chain, unable to reach anyone who passes by. She'll never be able to leave without me by her side. But, what am I thinking? She won't want to. I'll treat her nice. The glades are beautiful, full of wildlife. And, she'll love my home.*

***

Danni awoke early, dressed in her yellow and white floral bathing suit, and pulled on a pair of white capris and a cute yellow-scoop necked tee. She fastened a shell necklace on and automatically stuffed her driver's license, credit card, some cash, and her keys in her pocket. Opening the door, she stepped out and began walking toward the car. It was a gorgeous day. She wrinkled her nose and sniffed. Chloroform? She heard something move behind her. Pushed, she fell to the ground. A cloth covered the lower half of her face. A sickening smell flooded her senses.

She tried to push herself up, to get her feet under her. Dizzy, she fell forward and blacked out.

When she awakened, she was in the backseat of a car, gagged and blindfolded. She heard road noise, honking. When the honking stopped, she heard chewing and caught the scent of apples. Who had abducted her? Eddie? He liked apples. Who didn't? Maybe her captor was someone he'd hired? Or, someone else. Someone who had kidnapped her for ransom. Was she in danger? She'd be stupid to think she wasn't. Would she survive the ordeal? One way or another. She didn't dare allow herself to think that she might not.

She was stiff from being bound. Gagged and blindfolded, she couldn't speak, nor could she see. She wished to God the car would stop, but at least she was in the back seat covered with what she thought was a blanket. He or she hadn't tossed her in the trunk.

The car slowed and stopped, and she heard the front door open, then a gate squeaking and scraping on asphalt. The driver got in, shut the car door, and the car began to move. The car stopped again, the driver got out to apparently shut the gate, then came back and drove for a minute or so. After they stopped and the driver stepped out, the door next to her opened. Her abductor removed the blindfold, then the gag, and finally the tape that she'd been bound with.

She rolled over to face her abductor. "You!"

"I told you I'd see you soon," he said with a huge grin on his face.

She stared up at him. The sun reflected upon his curly, sandy hair, kissing it with shiny, light blond highlights. Tall and lean with a runner's physique, he was tan, with a medium brown mustache highlighted by the sun. His dimples shone as he smiled down upon her in triumph.

Who would have known that within this incredibly handsome man lurked the soul of an insane psychopath? The dark aviation sunglasses that he wore bestowed an aura of glamour and mystery to his persona, while masking his flat soulless eyes.

She was going to need to tread lightly. "Why did you kidnap me?"

"You're always leaving me," Eddie said. "What else was I to do?"

"I didn't really want to give up my home, but I didn't know what else to do."

"I know. You've been held prisoner and dictated to by your partner. But this time, he doesn't know you're with me, and he won't know for a while, if ever. There's no way he can find you. I know he was telling you what to do."

"Technically, since Vince died, he's my boss."

"That's not what I mean and you know it. Sweet Danni. I don't blame you. You've only been doing what you had to. And you're still mourning your husband even though he was a jerk. Don't worry. You'll be happy here. No one will bother you. We have guards."

"Guards?"

"Let me show you around. Take my hand so you don't trip. Your legs will be stiff from riding in the car so long, bound with tape as you were. We'll check out the grounds before we go inside. Stay with me and watch where you're walking. Be careful of the snakes and 'gators. There are a few panthers and a bear or two that cross over once in a while."

She was going to have to take his hand if she wanted to live. Clearly, in this case, co-operation was the ticket for a longer life.

"Okay. I don't think I want to meet any of those creatures up close and personal."

Eddie walked her down the path through the thick glades to

a canal, where a small boat was tied to a dock.

"It's beautiful here," she commented.

"Dangerous, too," Eddie added. "It's not usually so overgrown, but no one's been here for a while, and it doesn't take long in the semi-tropics to become a jungle."

"We're a long way from civilization, aren't we?"

"There's a small town nearby. It doesn't offer much, but there's a museum and a few shops. Once you're settled in, I'll take you there. I want you to see the beautiful little white church in the center of town. We'll be getting married there once your grieving period is over."

She wanted to push him away and run as fast as she could and as far away as she could. No way would she ever marry him. She had to escape.

Eddie glanced at her. "You're pale. Are you feeling all right?"

She nodded. "It's just hot." She rubbed the back of her neck.

"We'll come back later this afternoon when there's a sunset. We'll go to the house now so that I can show you around and you can rest for a while."

From the canal they took a boardwalk back. High above the swamps, she saw gators of all sizes sunning on the banks, waiting for prey that would be appetizers.

"You don't want to be here when the storms come. The swamps and canals flood, especially during hurricanes."

"I wouldn't want to be here then."

"No one would. If the hurricane doesn't get you, the 'gators will." He giggled.

Danni shuddered. She wondered if Eddie had ever left anyone bound and gagged in the house during a hurricane.

"We're nearly at the house. Stay close to me. The guards are out."

Danni saw them at a distance. A shiver ran up her spine.

155

"The pit bull at the back door is Ralph. The other is Henry. They're always irritable and hungry, especially so now. I don't know how much they've eaten in the past few days. When I'm here, I exercise and feed them. No one will bother us."

"No. I don't think they will." She tried to conceal her panic, not only from Eddie, but from dogs that would catch the sour scent of fear.

"You must be tired and hungry. I'll show you the gardens tomorrow."

"Gardens?"

Eddie laughed. "Of course. I'm a landscaper, remember? You hired me."

"I just didn't expect to find a garden in the middle of all of this wild beauty."

"After you see what I've done, you'll be proud of me. The grounds are a little overgrown now, but we'll be here for a while."

"Have you had this place long?"

"My oldest foster brother left it to me in his will," Eddie said. "He was one of the few people in my past that really liked me. He died young."

"From an accident?"

"Um…you might say that. He was shot."

"I'm sorry."

"So am I. I've missed him. It can get pretty lonely out here by yourself."

"I expect so. Is this all your land?"

"Mostly. It's a little over three acres," he said, unlocking a chain link fence. "I put the fence up to keep out the 'gators, panthers, and bears, among other things."

She nodded.

"The house isn't very large, just enough room for four or five people."

On stilts, it was a hexagon-shaped cedar and glass home with a tin roof. Lush vegetation and bright pink bougainvillea surrounded it. Walking far to the side of the dogs, they climbed up a doublewide stairway to a wraparound porch.

"It's okay to come out on the porch to read, sun, or to watch the sunsets, but don't ever go down the stairway without me. There's also a room downstairs, a storeroom on the ground floor, but Jake, a chow, and the meanest of the dogs, guards that area. Avoid it."

"I will. The house is beautiful, Eddie."

"Thanks. That's a real compliment, and I appreciate it. Lou, my foster brother, and I built it a couple of years before he was killed. There are many windows, but we added roll down hurricane shutters on each of them. The house and the grounds take a beating in the summers when the storms plow through."

"I imagine." *What a shame that Eddie is mentally ill. He could have had a wonderful career. Maybe, with medication and proper therapy, he still could. But, what am I thinking? He's a killer and he's going to fry when he's caught, unless he gets off a murder charge by a plea of insanity.*

"What are you thinking?"

"Just how versatile and talented you are. Your foster brother must have been the same."

"He was. Wait until you see the woodwork he did inside," Eddie said proudly.

Eddie unlocked the carved wooden door and led her inside. The house was light and bright. Plantation shutters hung by each window, while the floors were Saltillo tile. The walls were paneled in cypress. A grand piano rested in a corner of the living room.

"Do you play the piano, Eddie?"

"Some."

157

"I'd like to hear you play sometime."

"You will. Lou was the most talented of all of my foster brothers and sisters. In fact, sometimes during tourist season, he worked gigs in clubs on Marco Island."

"And you?"

"I play the guitar fairly well. I'll take a gig in Miami or Ft. Lauderdale now and then. What about you?"

"A little piano, that's it."

"Ever play professionally?"

She nodded. "Years ago, when I lived in New Orleans."

"You should have been with me a long time ago, you know that?"

Danni forced a smile. *No, Eddie. Your foster parents should have made sure you received proper treatment. But, you can be so charming; they probably didn't know you were ill.*

"You know, you can never leave me. For now, you'll have your own room. But after we're married, you will be sharing my room and my bed with me."

Danni gulped. *What if I don't want to?*

"You have a funny look on your face. I hope you're not thinking of trying to escape. You can't do that, you know. You won't make it. My dogs are killers," he said with a giggle that held a note of hysteria.

Chilled, she realized he was about to flip out.

"Actually, Eddie, I was wondering where the bathrooms are."

He laughed harshly. "Sorry. I didn't mean to threaten you, but you did have an odd look on your face. The thing is, no one ever wanted me around long. My foster parents kept passing me off, and my girlfriends left or betrayed me, like Tiffany did. Do you know that I found her in bed with a guy the last time I went to see her?"

"No. I didn't know that. That's about the worst thing that can happen to a person."

"You must know how I feel, because even if you didn't catch your husband in the act, you know that he cheated on you."

"How do you know that?"

"I know everything about you, Danni."

Oh boy. I sure hope not.

"I learned not to trust people from an early age."

"I'm sorry."

"See. You do understand. We're going to get along just fine.

Until I can figure a way out of here. Right now, I'm high on the list of Jake's food chain.

CHAPTER 31
CLUES

Bobby awoke to the sound of knocking on the front door. He rose, slipped into a terrycloth bathrobe, and padded out to answer the door. Opening it, he found Pete on the doorstep, pacing back and forth while he ran his hands through his hair.

"Come in, Pete. What's wrong?"

"Danni was supposed to meet me this morning at Lido Beach near the refreshment building. I waited and waited. When she didn't arrive, I walked up and down the beach looking for her. After that, I called her cell phone, but no one answered. Is she here?"

Bobby shook his head. "I don't think so. I'll check and see if she's in her room."

Pete sat down in the leather sofa and waited. He was afraid the answer was going to be no.

"She's not in her room. She parked her car outside last night."

"It's here. But Danni's not."

"Maybe she forgot about meeting you this morning and took a walk around the neighborhood."

"That's not like her."

"No, it isn't," Bobby said. "But, before we call Sal or the police, let's check the sales office."

Pete's heart sank. "I have a bad feeling about this."

"Don't jump to conclusions. Wait here a minute and I'll slip into a pair of sweats and a shirt. I won't be long." He was back out in a second with the keys. "Let's go."

When they couldn't locate Danni, Pete called Officer Cummings while Bobby called Sal. After the allowed amount of time had passed to report a missing person, an all-points bulletin was issued. Danni's face was on the front of every newspaper from Pensacola to Jacksonville, and from Miami to Naples. Two photos of Eddie were posted, one with sunglasses, one without, illustrating his scar. He was noted as wanted by the police for questioning in the murder case of Tiffany Owens and the abduction of Danni.

Neither Sal, Bobby, nor Officer Cummings could guess exactly when, where, or how she'd been abducted. Everyone agreed that Eddie had kidnapped her.

A week went by without any news. Pete hadn't been able to eat much of anything, nor had he been able to sleep. Sal returned to the models in Sarasota and suggested that Pete go home to Tequesta to help Madison with the baby. Remembering the close resemblance between Madison and Danni, Pete agreed to do so provided Officer Cummings would allow him to return, which he promptly did. He was free now, and no longer considered a person of interest in the case.

Before Pete left, he asked Sal to call a meeting to include Officer Cummings, Bobby, and himself as soon as possible.

"Officer," Pete said, "have we traced the floral delivery down?"

He nodded. "Yes. One of the residents near the model saw the truck and remembered the florist's name. We checked with them. The order was called in from a florist with a Collier County prefix."

"Have your detectives traced it?"

"Not yet. But it's on their list of to-do items for the day."

"I'm good with computers and research," Pete said. "If you could give me the number, I'll track it down right away. At the same time, I'd like to thoroughly research Eddie Haywood, Tiffany, and finally, Danni. Have your detectives done that?"

"They've run a check on Eddie Haywood and Tiffany. However, go ahead and check them out again. You may find something they missed."

"I'll be going back to the other coast and, with your help; I would like to check out Eddie Haywood's residence in Pompano with you."

"We'll need a search warrant," Officer Cummings said.

"Can we get it?"

He nodded. "I'll present the case to the judge in that district. Eddie's wanted for questioning in both a murder and kidnapping. It should have already been done. Someone slipped up."

"He may be keeping Danni in Pompano," Bobby suggested.

"I doubt it, but the search might lead us to where he does have her," Officer Cummings said.

"I'll leave this afternoon. Keep in touch," Pete said. "Let me know the earliest possible date that we can do the search."

***

The following day, Officer Cummings met Pete at Eddie's apartment in Pompano Beach after he had spoken with the judge and received a search warrant. Entering, it looked like an ordinary sparsely furnished apartment...plain, a few seascapes, and a tropical landscape. Nothing personal was in the living room except for a couple of newspapers and magazines.

They moved into the bedroom. A life-sized photo of Danni in a bikini swimsuit was tacked to the wall opposite the queen-sized bed. Other smaller photos of beautiful young women, dressed either in sheer lingerie or thongs and bras, were displayed.

"I'll need to find out who these women are or were," Officer Cummings said, taking photos of the wall. "I have a bad feeling that I'm going to find them among the missing person's files."

"I hope to God that they didn't meet their end like Tiffany did," Pete said. How long could Danni survive being held captive by a madman?

"You don't feel so good, do you, Pete? You're looking a little green."

His stomach was rolling. "I don't feel so great. I don't like where my thoughts are leading me."

"What we're looking for are clues to find Danni. Let's not assume anything drastic yet."

When they left the apartment, Pete asked, "Do you think it was worth your trip?"

"Damn right. Did you check out his magazines?"

Pete nodded. "Yeah, but all I saw was a lot of stuff on plants and landscaping. Oh yeah. There was a music magazine, too; guitars, I think."

"And magazines on plants and herbs. Some of which may be poisonous," Officer Cummings said. "I saw a couple of other things of interest, too."

"What's that?"

"A couple of matchbooks. One was from a restaurant in Marco Island, one from Bonita Springs, and one more from an ice cream place in Everglades City."

"Huh! Did you notice the photographs?" Pete asked.

"Didn't really focus on those, except for the photos of the girls."

"There are a couple of photos of the glades by Clyde Butcher. The guy's famous for his work in the Everglades."

"Where's he live?"

"Somewhere in Collier County, I think. He has a gallery in Ochopee and one in Venice."

"Ochopee, huh? That's close to Everglades City."

"Which is in Collier County, and was well known for its drug trade in the 70s and 80s. Didn't the florist in Sarasota say that the order for a dozen roses came from a number in Collier County…a 239 area code?" Pete asked.

"I think we're got something here."

"Collier County's a big place."

"But Ochopee isn't," Officer Cummings said. "Neither is Everglades City. Damn, I wish you lived in Sarasota County. Ever thought of being a police detective?"

Pete laughed. "No. I'm an artist."

"And talented or lucky with finances."

"Yeah, well, I've got to make a living. And the thing about police work is, you're not paid enough."

"Maybe not, but we take the bad guys off the streets and save women like Danni every day. It makes it all worth it."

"Let's just hope we can get to her before this nut case freaks out."

Pete's cell phone rang. It was Sal. Bobby had called and told them he had a strong feeling that Danni was in south Florida very close to Naples; somewhere off Tamiami Trail, which is also known as Highway #41.

"Where did he get that information?"

Pete listened to what Sal said, drew his brows together, and put him on hold.

"Officer, you might want to check out the area between the intersection of Highway 92 and Tamiami Trail to Everglades City. Bobby thinks she is being held in a house about three miles off Tamiami Trail."

Officer Cummings nodded. "Man! I don't know where he got that information, but I'll get right on it."

CHAPTER 32
DANNI'S ESCAPE

Danni sat in one of the big wicker chairs on the front porch, browsing through a fashion magazine that Eddie had given to her. She'd been at the bungalow for a week. So far, she'd been able to handle him. But, how much longer would she be able to?

In exchange for cooking three meals a day and light housecleaning, he'd seen to it that she had clean clothing to wear. Granted, the clothes were a size larger than she usually wore, but they covered her and she was grateful for that. She wondered who the clothing had belonged to. Tiffany? The very thought of wearing a dead girl's clothes gave her the creeps.

For the past week, she'd been watching Eddie closely and noted his habits, especially the door he left by, when he went out, and where he put his keys when he came in. Man-eating dogs or not, she intended to take her first opportunity to escape; on foot, by bike, or by car. She figured that the back door through the storeroom was the only safe way to go, since Eddie always left that way.

It was late in the afternoon, hot, steamy, and humid. Eddie had been irritable. She'd been trying to avoid him as much as possible. She wasn't sure what was wrong, but she'd heard him pacing back and forth last night. She'd awakened late, in the middle of the night, and had heard him just outside her door. He was crying and talking to himself.

"She's going to be like all the others. I know it. Tomorrow will be another day. Not a day like any others, but the day that will decide her fate."

***

The sun hung low in the tropical sky, nearly a quarter of the way to the horizon. Soon, Eddie would awaken from his afternoon nap and want coffee and cake, or brownies. Danni set her book down and moved into the kitchen to brew fresh coffee.

"I smell coffee. What did you make for us this afternoon?"

"Chocolate brownies. Sound good to you?"

"Great! Wrap some up for me. I'll be leaving around five-thirty. Make a steak sandwich too. You did keep the leftovers from last night, didn't you?'

"Sure, Eddie. I know how much you like cold steak sandwiches."

"I may be gone for a couple of days, but you'll be okay. There's plenty of food, books, and videos to entertain you. Mark, a friend of mine from Miami, will be in later this evening. He can stay in my room while I'm gone. I've told him to leave you alone, that you are my woman."

She nodded. "What about the dogs? Who will feed them?"

"Mark knows what to do."

She nodded. "All right then." She drew her brows together. "What happened to your arm?"

"I cut it."

"I can clean the wound and rewrap it before you go."

"It's okay. I'll have it looked at in the clinic down the road. Thanks for offering. You're not going to try to leave, are you?"

Danni shook her head. *No. I'm not going to try. I'm going to.*

"I don't know why you would want to. You have everything

166

you need right here. Mark's not a bad guy, so don't be afraid of him."

"All right. Would you mind if I play the piano while you're gone?"

"Feel free. Do anything you want to…cook, bake, read, whatever; just stay here and don't step off the porch. You can use the treadmill and the other workout equipment. When I get back, maybe we'll go to the little town down the road, or maybe fishing…just you and me."

"That would be nice."

After Eddie had finished his coffee and brownie, he went into his room. A half-hour or so later, he came back into the kitchen with a small bag. "I'll be going now. Tell Mark I'll give him a buzz later."

"Be sure to have your arm looked at. It might get infected."

"Sure. Hey! You're making me feel like you really care about me."

"Don't forget your steak sandwich," she said, handing him a brown paper lunch bag. "I put a bottle of water and a small bag of chips in, too."

Eddie's face lit up. "Thanks. That was really nice of you."

"Bye, Eddie."

He turned, waved, and shut the door.

She waited fifteen minutes. Eddie didn't return. She moved into the room that she'd been staying in, changed into a pair of jeans, a shirt, and tennis shoes. Taking her driver's license, credit card, money, and the keys to the model in Sarasota that she'd hidden, she stuffed them into her pocket. Grabbing a black, shiny tote bag, which was in the closet, she tossed in a pair of clean underwear, the white capri's and tee she'd arrived in, as well as lipstick gloss and a hairbrush. Moving into the kitchen, she opened one of the drawers and tossed a flashlight in the tote, as well as a couple of apples and granola bars.

She'd seen him put his keys on the kitchen table. They were gone now. But, a couple of days ago, he'd hung a set of keys on a hook just inside the pantry. Surely he couldn't have forgotten and left them there. If he had, she was in luck! If not, well, she'd thumb it to Naples. He believed she'd fallen for the tale that Jake would devour her. She'd stake her life on the fact that he was on a short line. Opening the pantry, her eyes widened. She smiled. A set of keys hung on the hook. She glanced out of the window. He'd taken the truck.

Thinking of Jake, she opened the lid to the kitchen wastebasket, removed the steak bone, and wrapped it loosely. With the tote bag hitched over her shoulder, the treat for Jake in one hand, and the keys, which she hoped were to Eddie's car, in the other hand, she moved down the stairway to the storeroom. Taking a deep breath, she gulped and moved to the door that led outside. Turning the dead bolt, she cautiously opened the door.

Jake was asleep. Halfway to the car, she glanced up. The dog opened an eye. Growling, he rose, stood, and licked his chops. He barked, and broke into a run. *Uh-oh. Maybe the chain's not so short.* Her heartbeat quickened. Jake looked hungry. She paused, threw the bone, turned, ran, and clicked the fob. What if Eddie hadn't taken the car because the battery was dead? Beads of perspiration broke out on her brow. The sour acidic scent of fear filled the air. The chow knew she was afraid, but she hoped the bone had distracted him, if only for a few minutes. The lock clicked. The lights flashed on. Danni kept running. Her mouth was dry. Her heart hammered when she reached for the handle of the car door. Opening it, she stepped in and slammed the door behind her. She exhaled a deep breath, glanced up, and saw that Jake was chewing on the bone. She started the engine, raced out of the driveway, and onto the road.

She turned onto the paved road as fast as she could safely do so. Hoping the road would lead to a highway, she drove straight. When she reached a wide rusty gate with an X in the center, she moved the gear into park, slid out of the seat, and with a sense of triumph, opened the gate. Not bothering to close it, she returned to the car, slid in, and slammed the door shut again. She made a left hand turn onto a highway, which she hoped was Highway 41.

She ran her fingers through her hair and pressed down on the accelerator. Her biggest fear was that she might run into Eddie on the highway. What if he'd forgotten something? If he caught her, she had no doubt that she would end up like Tiffany. A loud horn sounded behind her. Gulping, she glanced in the rear view mirror. Not Eddie; a huge black pickup was on her tail. Thinking the driver more than likely wanted to pass; she slowed and moved slightly to the right of the road. He honked again, passed, and sped down the road.

Her nerves were on edge. She couldn't relax until she was safe. When would that be?

Turning on the radio to take her mind off Eddie, the tune, "I Can See Clearly Now," by Jonny Nash drifted through the car. She took it to be a good sign; a signal that she was free.

Chapter 33
The Blowout

Bang! The car bucked, and the steering wheel shook. Danni took her foot off the accelerator, didn't brake, but slowed and allowed the car to roll to a stop.

Damn! A blowout!

Danni opened the car door and stepped out, and circling the car, discovered that the left rear tire had blown. Opening the trunk, she prayed that Eddie had a spare and tools with which to change the tire.

A truck honked. She heard it pull over just behind her. Her heart jumped to her throat. Eddie?

She turned around. A red Dodge pick-up with a Native American woman had pulled over just behind her. She climbed out of the pick-up and moved toward her. Wearing worn jeans and a pretty sky blue shirt, she asked, "Do you need help, honey?"

Danni's eyes filled with tears. Thank God.

"Actually, I do. It's been a long time since I've changed a tire."

"Maybe never?"

"Mmm…my husband demonstrated the process, but I've never changed a tire myself."

"Then, we'll do it together. The first thing we do after we remove the spare and the tools is loosen the lug nuts on the tire.

You do that and I'll do the next step."

Danni loosened the lug nuts.

"Okay. Now, I'm going to jack up the car nearest the flat and raise the car enough so that the tire is at least one inch clear of the ground."

"What do we do now?" Danni asked as traffic whizzed by.

"Now you can remove the lug nuts that you loosened."

"That was easy."

"What I'm going to do now," Mollie said, "Is remove the tire by pulling it directly toward me."

The tire came off easily, but Danni frowned. "What if that motion makes the jack collapse and the car falls?"

"We just pray that it doesn't. But, I never place my legs or limbs under the car when I'm doing that. It's your turn now. Just put on the spare."

Danni picked it up, moved closer, and placed the spare on. "Whew!"

"Now, you go ahead and tighten the lug nuts a little and then I'll jack the car down."

Danni did so. By this time, her hands were black and she had black streaks on her cheeks and forehead where she'd touched her face.

After the car was jacked down, Mollie tightened the lug nuts.

"We did it, girl! You've just changed your first tire."

"With a lot of help from you. I couldn't have done it otherwise," Danni said.

"I'm Mollie," the Native American woman said.

"And I'm Danni."

"I'm on my way into Naples. Where are you going?"

"To the first fire station that I come to."

"What's wrong?"

Danni sighed. "I've been held prisoner in the glades by a

man with vicious dogs guarding me. I just escaped. It's the first chance I've had, and I've been afraid all this time that one of the trucks that passed us would be him looking for me."

"My Lord. You do look familiar. In fact, you're the girl that's been in all of the papers for over a week. Why, half of the United States is looking for you. You must be the widow from the Boca Raton area."

Danni nodded. Tears ran down her cheeks.

"Just climb in my truck, honey. We'll leave your jailers car here by the side of the road. If he passes us, he won't recognize my truck. In fact, I'll take you to the police station where you should be going, then you can tell them all about the jerk that kidnapped you. He needs to be caught before he hurts more women."

A highway sign in front of them warned Slow. Panther Crossing Ahead. Danni had been here before on her way from Miami to Naples. The corners of her mouth tilted up. They were traveling west on Highway 41, close to, or in, Big Cypress Preserve, just outside of Naples. Mollie slowed, and then braked. In front of the truck, not more than five-hundred feet ahead, a huge cat darted across the road, tan in color. Danni's heart lightened, knowing it was one of Florida's near extinct panthers.

"I love those cats," Mollie said.

"This is my lucky day," Danni said.

"And it's going to continue on like this," Mollie said.

After Mollie stopped the pick-up in front of the Naples Police Station, Danni climbed out, clutching the tote that she'd taken from Eddie's house. "Thank you so much, Mollie. I hope we meet again someday."

"So do I."

"You can find me through the JVS development office in Boca. Just ask for Danni Giardini."

"Expect a call from me one of these days. I'd like you to come

172

out to the reservation and meet my family."

"I'd love to."

"Now, go on in and tell your story."

Danni turned, waved, and walked on into the station.

***

An hour and a half later, Pete rushed into the station to retrieve Danni. She had already given the police all of the information that they needed and was waiting for someone to pick her up. She'd had some time after she had been interrogated, and had washed her face and cleaned up the best she could. She wasn't sure, but she thought that Officer Cummings would be driving in from Sarasota and picking her up.

"Oh, thank God, you're here. How did you find me?"

"The Naples police called Officer Joe Cummings, who called me," he said, hugging her tight. "We've been looking all over for you. I was down in Everglades City this afternoon checking with the florist that took the order for the flowers that Eddie sent to you, so Joe asked me to pick you up here since I was in the general area."

"What flowers?"

"I forgot. You weren't there when they were delivered. Eddie sent you flowers before he kidnapped you, with a note saying that he would see you soon. I traced the order to a florist in Everglades City. This morning I drove down to talk to them. I just saw Eddie's car parked by the side of the road on Highway 41."

"I was driving it and had a blowout. I'll tell you all about my escape later. A woman from the Seminole Tribe saw me by the side of the road, helped me change the tire, and brought me here when she recognized me as the woman who had been missing. She saw my picture in the paper."

Pete nodded. "You've become famous."

Danni chuckled. "I once wanted fame, but not in the way that I gained it."

"We've been looking for Eddie's car and his pickup. I had both of the license plate numbers with me, so I recognized his car."

"I'm so glad to see you. I didn't think I was ever going to be able to get away from Eddie. It was awful. He didn't hurt me, but I was edgy every minute. If I didn't do exactly as he asked, I knew that I'd end up being food for Jake, Eddie's meanest dog." Danni sighed. "I'm so tired. I told the police the story."

"Where is Eddie now?"

"I don't know. He headed out about a few hours ago and left me alone with the dogs. A friend of his is on his way in from Miami. I'm afraid no one will be able to find Eddie. He's so crazy, Pete. He needs psychological help more than I can say."

"Do you have any idea where Eddie went?"

"I think he was on his way to his apartment in Pompano. He cut his arm last night, so he may be going to a medical clinic in a little town not far from where he lives in the glades."

"Everglades City?"

"I think so. I don't think he thought I would try to escape; not with his horrible dogs guarding the house."

CHAPTER 34
EDDIE RUNS

Eddie placed his forefingers to his temples. His headache was getting worse and his arm hurt like hell. He couldn't pull over to rest. He had to go on, pick up a few belongings in his apartment, and take the pictures of the dead girls off the wall. They'd deserved their fate. All of them had either deserted him or betrayed him, all but Danni. He'd had to leave her, put some distance between them. He didn't want to hurt her, but he knew that eventually, he would.

Danni was an innocent, and even though he knew Sal wanted her, he knew in his heart that she'd been true to Vince. When he'd been standing outside her door last night, he could have sworn he'd heard a voice, maybe his inner voice, telling him to leave her alone, to let her go.

The police were looking for him. They suspected or knew that he'd killed Tiffany and had taken Danni. If he left Florida, they'd never find him. He might have borrowed some time by growing a beard, but not much. If they stopped him and recognized him, they would arrest him. If they managed to convict him of Tiffany's murder, he'd fry. *No way, dude. It's not worth taking a chance. I'm headed to my bud's in Giddings, Texas. They'll never trace me to his house…haven't been there since I was a kid.*

175

An hour later, Eddie pulled up in front of his apartment. At least now he could clean out his wound again, rewrap it, get some sleep, and head out in the morning. When he opened the door to the apartment, he knew someone had been here. For one, things were out of place; there was dirt on the floor. *All right, so I won't be able to rest. Not here.*

Moving into the bedroom, he grabbed his bag and stuffed it full. *What the hell? I won't be coming back.* He grabbed the photos of Danni and left the rest. Whoever had been in the apartment had already seen the wall.

Forget sleeping. He had to go on. He dumped the bottles in his medicine cabinet and his shaving stuff in a paper bag. When he was ready to leave, he washed his face, poured peroxide on his arm, rebandaged it, and took a couple of aspirin. He grabbed his bags and headed out, not stopping until he was well out of the state of Florida. He found a walk-in clinic in Biloxi, Mississippi, the next day. He parked, went in, and had his arm attended to.

CHAPTER 35
A ROMANTIC INTERLUDE

Pete's cell phone rang. Sal's number appeared on the small screen. He placed it on speaker phone so that Danni could talk to him.

"Hello, Sal."

"Joe Cummings called me. Have you seen Danni yet?"

"I'm right here, Sal. As I told Pete, it's a long story, but I managed to escape. I'm safe now and I've told the police all about my episode and where I believe Eddie is now."

"Thank God. We were afraid we would never see you again."

"There were a few times that I might have agreed with you," Danni said.

"Look, I'm not going to be able to fly over to Naples tonight, but I'll be there by noon tomorrow. I've already booked a couple of suites for us in Naples. I'm bringing some clothes over for you."

"You didn't need to make reservations for us. We could easily just drive into Sarasota and stay in the model. I have clothes there."

"No. You can't do that. We're not in the model any longer. Pete will fill you in."

"But, I'm not dressed for a nice hotel. I only have what I'm wearing, along with capris that I brought with me in a tote bag. They're not appropriate for much of anything."

Sal laughed. "I'm sure whatever you have on is just fine to check in."

Danni glanced at Pete and wrinkled her nose. "I suppose so."

Pete heard her unspoken words. She felt dirty, wanted to take a shower, wash her hair, and eat. He would like to take her out for a nice dinner with soft music, but he didn't think she would be up to it.

"Okay then. I'll see you two tomorrow."

Pete clicked off.

"I really don't want to go to the hotel looking like this. I wish that Sal wouldn't have made reservations at such an upscale hotel."

"The department stores are still open. We can stop by the shopping center before we check in if you would like to," Pete said. "It'll be on me."

"That's thoughtful of you, Pete. I really would like to do that. I need some cosmetics and a few other things that I doubt Sal will think of."

"No problem, but I'm going to stick by you every minute. I'm not going to take any chances with you from now on. Eddie's full of too many tricks, and you're one of the most impulsive people I've ever known."

The corners of Danni's mouth tilted up in a beautiful smile. "Lingerie department first."

"Do I get to help you choose?" Pete asked with a wide grin and a twinkle in his eyes.

"Sure, why not. Just no polka dots!"

"I hate the polka dot pajamas and bikinis that my cousin wears," Pete said, laughing.

"You mean Madison?"

"Uh-huh."

"I think I have one of her polka dot bikinis. I found it in Vince's gym bag when I was clearing his things out."

"I'm sorry to remind you of that. I wasn't thinking."

"It's no problem, Pete. Although I'd like to have a few words with him about the poor choices he made, I've forgiven him for his infidelities. I will try to remember only the good times that we had together. Because of his betrayal, a new spirit entered the world, one that we will all love."

"You're amazing." Pete pulled into the parking lot. "Let's see how much damage you can do in just an hour or so."

Forty minutes later, loaded down with packages, Danni glanced up at Pete and smiled. "Thanks for your help. You're fun to shop with, and we found some things for you, too."

"Anytime. It was a pleasure. I particularly enjoyed seeing you model the dinner dress for me. I only wish you would have modeled the black silk nightgown that I chose for you." Pete turned and flashed a rakish smile.

Danni poked him in the ribs playfully with her elbow and laughed. "I'll just bet you do. After we check in and I make myself beautiful, do you suppose we could go out for cocktails?"

He chuckled. "Change into one of those dynamite cocktail dresses and we'll have dinner too…that is, if you're up to it. You've had a trying day."

"But I have my life back now."

"Thank God!"

***

After they had checked in, showered, and dressed, Pete's cell phone rang. It was Sal again. Pete answered, listened, and his face broke into a wide grin. "Well, darlin', it looks like I have you all to myself not only tonight, but tomorrow morning too. You look stunning." Pete eyes sparkled as his eyes traveled over her dynamite figure. "Sal said he wasn't sure when he would be arriving. It could be anywhere from tomorrow around noon to mid-afternoon. He hasn't been able to contact his pilot."

"Hmm. If I know Sal and he wants to come over tomorrow morning, he'll drive if he can't locate the pilot." *Once he begins thinking about Pete and I alone together, he'll be in his car in a minute.*

"You're probably right about that."

"Why didn't you stay at the model?"

"Joe Cummings released me and I went back to Tequesta to keep an eye on Madison and the baby. You know, you two do resemble each other, and I was concerned about that."

"Do we really look that much alike?"

"Not enough to be twins, but enough to be mistaken for the other, especially at a distance. After I went back to the other coast, both Sal and Bobby returned too."

"But what about my car and the clothes that I had at the model?"

"Sal took your things back to the other coast and has them at his place in Boca. Bobby drove your car back to the other coast and parked it at Sal's."

"Wow! If I hadn't had the blow out and met Mollie, the woman who helped me with the tire, I might have decided to go on in to Sarasota. It would have been for nothing."

Pete's brow shot up. "Tell me that you didn't really consider driving Eddie's car that far by yourself. He might have seen you. We don't know where he is."

"It was only a thought."

"A dangerous one. I'm really glad to see you. You have no idea of how worried we've all been. You're safe with me, and I'm looking forward to being alone with you tonight...and if I'm really lucky, tomorrow morning too."

Danni's smile reached her eyes. "I don't think I've had the

pleasure of being alone with you since I ran into you in Palm Beach."

"It's not because I didn't want to. When your divorce is final, we'll make up for all of that lost time, darlin'."

The corners of her mouth turned up. "I'll look forward to it."

***

After having escaped from Eddie's home in the Everglades where she'd been held captive for more than a week, being questioned by the police about Eddie, and her nerve-wracking experience in the glades with him, Danni was exhausted by the time she and Pete had finished dinner.

"You're tired, aren't you?"

"Yes. But this evening has been perfect. After a week and a half of remaining alert at all times and sleeping with one eye open, you've brought happiness back into my life."

"I'm glad to hear that. Would you like to call it an evening?"

"That's probably a good idea. Usually I have more energy."

"It's all right, darlin.' Sal will, more than likely, be here first thing in the morning."

***

After returning to the suite, they discovered that they were alone. Danni and Pete said their goodnights and moved into their separate suites.

Danni awoke in the middle of the night, tossing and turning. Thinking she was still at Eddie's, she sat up and took note of her surroundings. Then she remembered. She'd escaped. She was safe. Pete was in the other suite. She rose, slipped into the hotel robe, and moved into the kitchen, where she took a bottle of water from the fridge and set it on the counter.

"Couldn't sleep?" she heard Pete ask behind her. "Neither could I."

She turned to face him and said, "I slept for a while, but then

I had a bad dream. I thought I was back at Eddie's and woke up."

Pete drew her close and whispered, "Don't worry, darlin', you're with me now."

She laid her head on his shoulder, hugged him, and said softly, "I know."

"I thought I'd lost you," he murmured.

"I must admit, it was touch and go."

The sound of a key sliding into the lock of the door to the suite jarred them.

"Who do you think it is?

"Someone who's at the wrong room...probably drunk," Pete said.

"I think it's Sal. I think he drove over in his Porsche."

"Better go to your room."

She giggled. "It's late. Think he might be jealous?"

"He knows me better than that. And aside from the fact that you've been recently widowed, I am a gentleman and you have been through a lot lately. That's not to say that I wouldn't like to ravish you. But, now is not the time."

Danni flashed him a wide smile and moved back into her room.

"See you in the morning, darlin'."

"Goodnight, Pete. Sweet dreams."

***

Sal set his luggage down, moved to the mini-bar, and selected the finest bourbon they stocked and proceeded to make himself a bourbon and water. He was tired and hadn't planned on coming over tonight, but he'd been concerned about Danni. He'd driven over in his Porsche.

The past week, with Danni missing, had been enough to drive a sane man over the edge. He was thankful to Pete for jumping in on the case with Joe Cummings, and for instigating the search of

Eddie's apartment. Last, but not least, Pete had followed down the clue that the florist had left. It was a stroke of luck that Pete had seen Eddie's car enter Highway 41 late yesterday afternoon and followed.

He wondered how close Pete and Danni had become. He didn't think their relationship had developed further, not yet. Pete was an honorable man, from all that he'd seen. He wouldn't take advantage of Danni unless she wanted him to. He finished his drink. Rather than sleep in the other queen-sized bed in the room where Pete was sleeping, he pulled out the sofa bed in the sitting room and was asleep within minutes.

When the alarm went off in the morning, Danni shut it off and burrowed down into the covers and went back to sleep. Sal awoke early with a backache from the sofa that he'd slept on. He made coffee but decided not to disturb Danni until after he'd showered and dressed.

"Hey Sal. Good to see you. You made coffee!" Pete padded into the kitchen. "Is Danni up yet?"

"I think she's in the shower now. I ordered breakfast for all of us. It should be here soon."

"I'm starved. What did you order?"

"The usual…freshly squeezed orange juice, poached eggs with Canadian bacon, home fries, fruit, and English muffins. Does that sound okay to you?"

"Sounds great!"

"You are flying to Austin with us today, aren't you, Pete? We'll be taking the two-thirty flight from Ft. Myers."

"Actually, Sal, we'll need to cancel the reservations. Officer Cummings called me just after I spoke with you. He's driving down to Naples this morning, and wants to speak with Danni."

"I thought she had already spoken with the police here."

"She did, but Joe wants Danni to drive out with him to show

183

him exactly where Eddie held her hostage."

"Damn!"

"My thoughts too. I haven't told her yet. Personally, I think it's going to be too much for her emotionally."

Sal nodded. "I don't see why she can't just draw him a map. If Eddie came back and is there, it could be a disaster."

Pete exhaled a deep sigh. "I don't know how we can talk him out of it."

Sal shook his head. "We can't. But if he insists on this, then I think we should go along."

"Absolutely."

"I don't know about you, but I have a license to carry a concealed weapon."

"So do I."

"We don't need to let Joe know, but we should be armed."

"Damn right," Pete agreed. "What if Eddie is there and goes wacky? Or the other guy, Mark. We don't know who he is."

"A criminal, I'd bet. Maybe he brought someone else along too."

***

It was nearly noon by the time Officer Cummings called and informed them that he had arrived in Naples. They agreed to meet him at a coffee shop near Naples Beach.

Danni was reluctant and didn't like Joe's plans. In fact, when Sal told her of his plans, she refused. The only way she would agree was if she could ride with Pete in his car along with Sal, and only to the entrance where the gate was.

Joe didn't like the plan, but finally agreed.

"You shouldn't drive anywhere near that house without back up...not even down the drive."

Joe nodded. "I'll take that to heart. Let's have lunch, and by the time we're finished, I'll have all of the backup I need."

"Thank God."

"All right" Pete said. "Danni can point out the entrance. I'll drive right on down Highway 41 until we come to a turnaround, and head back to Naples to the hotel."

"And once we're in the hotel, I'm going to make reservations for the first plane out to Austin, where Danni will finally be safe. If there's nothing available, I'm calling my pilot and telling him to drop everything and fly us over."

"That'll work," Joe said.

"You will call us later," Danni said, "and let us know what went on."

"Sure will."

"Okay then. Good luck."

"And the same to you."

Danni was nervous all the way to Eddie's, constantly looking for his truck. She felt that this was going to be a disaster. Once she had pointed out Eddie's gate, gone on down the road a bit, and turned around, she began to tremble. A shot rang out, and then another. Her stomach churned.

Pete sped up, fearing the worst. As he neared the Naples city limits, two police cars passed them with their lights and sirens on. Following were two fire trucks and several ambulances.

"Damn. I'm glad you refused to go with Joe."

"I had a really bad feeling about it."

"Both Sal and I thought it was a really bad idea."

"While Pete's been driving, I've been checking flights on my iPod."

"Find anything?"

"Yeah. My pilot's going to pick us up at the Sarasota airport later this afternoon. We'll leave from there. Let's go pack our bags, check out, and get out of here."

"You're coming with us, aren't you, Pete?" Danni asked."

185

He nodded. "You need all the protection you can get. Madison and the baby will be okay until we can bring them to Austin." Pete's cell phone rang. He glanced at the screen. It was the Naples Police Department. "Pete here."

Danni glanced at Pete. He didn't have his speaker phone on, but she could tell by his expression that this was serious. He drew his brows together and said, "I'll tell her."

"What happened?"

Pete took a deep breath. "Joe was shot. He's in the hospital in surgery. Another officer was killed. No one saw Eddie at the house, but there were three men there. Mark, whom you spoke of, tore out the back as soon as the police pulled up, but not without shooting Officer Cummings first. He disappeared into the glades and no one has been able to find him. The other two men who were there were shot and killed. So were the dogs."

"Who were the other two men? Eddie only told me that Mark would be there."

"They were both from Miami...both were drug dealers and wanted by the Miami Police Department. One of them was wanted for rape and murder."

Danni paled. "I would have been raped and killed."

Pete nodded. "More than likely."

"Let's get Danni the hell out of here before something else happens," Sal said. "I'd sure like to have Madison and the baby join us in Austin. She's in danger, and not just from hurricanes. She looks way too much like you, Danni."

"I agree with you," Danni said. "They could be killed if they stay where they are in a cat.2 hurricane, and I certainly don't want Eddie mistaking her for me. I'm guessing that her friend will manage the bookstore."

"I expect so."

"Have you spoken with them about this, Pete? Sal?"

"I mentioned it to her yesterday," Sal said. "She was interested, but concerned about how you would feel about the situation."

"I don't know Madison yet, but she is more than likely concerned about whether I'm holding a grudge against her since she was my husband's, err...soon to be ex-husband's mistress. She had no idea Vince was married. And anyway, Pete, you are her cousin as well as one of my very good friends. I'm looking forward to playing with that adorable baby."

"I was hoping you would feel that way," Pete said, with a wide smile on his handsome face.

"Will we be looking for a large home near the lake for all of us?" Danni asked.

"I like that idea, but slightly modified," Sal said. "A home with a guest house for Madison and the baby would be preferable. We'll also need an office."

"Sounds perfect," Danni said. "Jazzy may know of something in either case."

"That leaves tonight and maybe tomorrow night. Where we stay depends...." Sal left his sentence unfinished.

"Upon what?"

"Who has rooms available? Jazzy isn't expecting us tonight, and I don't just want to drop in on her. I'd like to book suites for one or two nights at the Driskill Hotel in downtown Austin. It's one of the most well-known historical hotels in Texas."

"I've heard about it," Pete said. "If I remember correctly, it was built in 1886 as the showplace of cattle baron, Jessie Driskill. But, I don't need a suite. Just book a standard room for me."

"Sounds interesting. Book a single room for me, too. I don't need a suite either, Sal."

"Then I'll ask for three rooms. They will all be charged to the company."

187

Pete shook his head. "I'll pick up my own room."

"That's not necessary. You're already working for JVS doing the murals in the models. I insist. Please let the company pick up your room too."

"We'll see. There may not be anything available."

"Before you do that, I need to call Jazzy. If she's heard the news, she's probably frantic."

"No. She's not. I called her and told her you had escaped… that you were fine," Sal said. "But, I couldn't tell her exactly when we were arriving in Austin."

"Thanks. That was very thoughtful of you."

"The truth is, I had no choice. From the time that your disappearance became national news, Jazzy and your friends have been calling every day."

"I didn't know that."

"You might want to give Evelyn and Vivian a call."

"Lainey too," Pete said. "Running Deer called several times. I called him yesterday after you escaped."

"I'll call them tomorrow. So, it's the Driskill tonight!"

CHAPTER 36
A FORGOTTEN MEMORY

Bobby locked up the sales office and drove to the beach to check out the waves. Rarely did the Florida surf impress him. He knew within a couple of hours' flight time he could be in Costa Rica, or any of the Central America surf spots. Although he'd heard many great things about Austin as a city, he was indifferent about the prospect of starting a building operation there. It seemed to him that they were a couple of years too late. From all indications, it looked like the economy was heading south. Though they were still building, especially around the lake, there were many foreclosures. Those who could were leasing their homes. Unless Sal had something unusual planned that was desperately needed, Bobby didn't think he was going to make a profit of any kind for at least three or four years. But, as far as he was concerned, the change to Austin offered him a chance to travel to Mexico more, maybe even to Southern California.

Pulling into a parking spot, Bobby rolled his pants legs up, got out of the car, locked it, and headed toward the beach for a long walk. Something bothered him about the Austin idea, and it wasn't only the fact that he believed it was too late to begin development there. It was more personal. He shrugged his shoulders. He'd sleep on it. Whenever he had a problem, he simply let it rest until the following day. When he awoke, he always knew what to do to solve it. He bent down, picked up a pebble, stood, and cast it out to sea.

CHAPTER 37
AUSTIN

"Oh! This is beautiful. Just look at the columned lobby, the gorgeous marble floors, and the stained glass dome above!" Danni said, admiring her surroundings.

"Wow! This is as nice as The Grand Duchess."

"While you two admire the lobby, I'll check in," Sal said, moving to the registration desk.

"Sir, I'm sorry, but we don't have anything available."

"Is there something wrong?" Pete asked, approaching the desk.

"There's nothing available."

"Maybe you made the reservations under your own name instead of JVS," Danni suggested.

The reservation clerk checked. "Yes, ma'am. Mr. Catalano, we are holding three of our best rooms under your name. They are all close to each other and on the same floor. Would you like me to place them under JVS instead?"

"If you would, please."

"Would you like our valet to carry your bags to your rooms?"

"Great."

"I realize it's getting late, but we are all starved. Are you still serving dinner?" Danni asked.

191

"The dining room is closed, but you may either order room service or you may dine in the bar."

"I would really like to have dinner with both of you rather than alone in my room," Danni said."

"I'd like that too," Pete said.

"Why don't you two have dinner in the bar? Since I still have calls and work to do, I'll order from my room," Sal said.

"Shall we?" Pete asked.

Danni nodded. "I'm starved."

"I'll meet up with you in the morning for breakfast," Sal said.

CHAPTER 38
DINNER WITH PETE

After Pete and Danni had ordered food and drinks in the elegant lounge, Pete said, "I'm sure glad that the bar is still serving food."

"So am I."

"It's really nice having dinner alone with you again tonight."

The edges of Danni's lips turned up. "Thank you. I'm enjoying my freedom, and your company. If not for you, I might not be alive."

"Your escape from Eddie is due to your courage, darlin'. All I did was follow up on leads. Thank God for your intelligence and bravery."

"I took the first opportunity that presented itself to chance an escape. There wasn't a moment that I wasn't afraid. When I had the blowout, I was so thankful that Mollie, the Seminole woman, stopped to help. I didn't know exactly how to change a tire, and I was terrified that Eddie would pass by on his way back and see me. When Mollie recognized me, she refused to allow me to drive on alone and took me into the Naples Police Station. Your appearance there was so timely, I do believe that angels led you there."

"You were fortunate. Divine intervention must have played

a part in your escape. And now," he said, placing his hand over hers, "I am happy to be dining alone with you tonight."

"And I. You and Sal seem to have become friends. It's obvious that he trusts you."

"He has no reason not to; however, I'm sure he has guessed that when your divorce is final, darlin', I have every intention of pursuing you."

Danni smiled. "I'll look forward to it."

***

On the way back to their rooms, they discovered that Pete's room was next to hers on the second floor.

Pete drew his brows together. "I almost wish that we did have a suite. You had a nightmare last night. Are you going to be all right in a single room by yourself tonight?"

"I think so."

"Well, if not, feel free to knock on my door. I don't suppose we have connecting rooms."

"I don't know. Let's look."

Pete took her key and opened the door to the hotel room. It was beautiful, elegant, but it was not a connecting room to his.

"It's not, but I'm sure I'll be okay. I don't suppose Eddie is anywhere nearby."

After Pete had left, Danni took a hot bath, slipped into her new gown and robe, watched TV for about an hour, and fell asleep. During the middle of the night she dreamed of Eddie; dreamed that he'd followed her and was now sitting in the chair of her room watching her. She screamed, sat straight up in bed, her eyes wide open, and screamed again.

A loud knock came at the door.

Danni blinked her eyes. No one was in the chair. The light she'd left on in the bathroom dimly lit the room. She slipped into the robe and moved to the door.

"Who is it?"

"Pete. I heard you scream. Is everything all right?"

"Yes. I just had a nightmare."

"Do you want to come to my room? There's another bed in there… two doubles."

"Thanks, but I'll be okay."

"Okay, but if it happens again, don't hesitate," Pete said.

"All right."

"Good night, then."

"Good night, Pete."

For the balance of the night Danni slept soundly, undisturbed by nightmares. The next morning, Pete and Danni joined Sal for breakfast and decided to drive to Lakeway.

CHAPTER 39
THE LAKE

Sal followed directions as Jazzy had instructed. When he reached a deli, he pulled in.

"I'm going in to for a newspaper. Would either of you like a cup of coffee?"

"Please."

"Me too."

"What do you think about the area?" Pete asked.

"I think it's already been done, as far as building is concerned. And I'm wondering two things," Danni said. "One, where's the lake? Secondly, except for the downtown area, I haven't seen any hotels. Where are they?"

"I've been wondering the same thing. The hills are beautiful. I wouldn't have expected it of Texas. In fact, this area reminds me a little of California. So far, I haven't seen any galleries."

"Neither have I, but we've been on freeways."

"Not exactly a great way to sightsee. Hey. I wasn't thinking. I'd better give Sal a hand."

"If you see anything good to eat, like cookies or whatever, please pick some up for us."

***

Sal and Pete returned to the car carrying cups of coffee. Plastic bags full of groceries were looped over their arms.

"What did you buy?"

"I called Jazzy for further directions. She suggested that I pick up steaks and chicken breasts to grill tonight. Man, they have a great deli and meat market."

"What else do you have?"

"Stuffed baked potatoes from the deli, and a dessert from the bakery."

"Sounds yummy," she said, taking a bag from Pete as well as a cup of coffee.

"Jazzy's house isn't far. It's on a cliff overlooking the lake with a view from three angles."

"Nice," Pete commented.

"Picturesque."

"One of the first things that I need to do is to find the local art supply," Pete said. "Wish I'd brought my oils and canvasses."

"Hmmm. Since no one will need my help as far as my secretarial skills or designer talents are concerned, maybe I'd better plan on picking up some note paper to outline a few articles."

"Good idea, Danni. If you need a couple of sketches or an illustrator, I can do that too."

"Thanks, Pete."

As they approached, Sal said, "Perfect. This calls for a boat. I'd heard Austin had received more than its share of rain. The lake's full."

"Madison's going to love this."

CHAPTER 40
MISSING INFORMATION

The waves rolled in, well-formed and breaking cleanly. It was a great day for surfing in southeast Florida. Bobby caught his last wave of the day and was riding it in. When he reached the shoreline, he set his board down and gazed out to sea, thinking of something he'd heard at the office.

Danni, Sal, and Pete had left for Austin a month ago. Since then, he'd been trying to remember what it was. It had to do with his lack of comfort over their leaving for Texas. Yesterday, he'd taken Madison and the baby to the airport to join them for the summer. In doing so, he'd inadvertently placed her in grave danger. She was not Danni's twin by a long shot. But, from the back, and from a distance, they resembled each other.

He dried off, tossed the towel down on the sand, and sat down. A couple of months ago, Eddie had come into the office to pick up his check. He'd been dressed in jeans, a Western-style shirt, and Western boots. Most of the time he wore shorts and a T-shirt and tennis shoes.

"Hey, Eddie. Cool boots! New for you, aren't they?"

"No, kid. Up until the time I was about ten or twelve, I lived with my foster parents on a small ranch in Giddings, Texas, not far from Austin. I did some riding, a little calf roping, and belonged to 4-H."

"Get outta' here."

"No, dude. I'm taking my girl to a rodeo this weekend in Arcadia."

***

Bobby rose, grabbed his towel and surfboard, and went back to Sal's place where he'd been staying. He showered and dressed, and then called Sal. There was no answer. He tried Pete and Danni. No one answered. He left a voice mail for each of them. As an afterthought, he called Officer Joe Cummings, the detective in Sarasota that had been working on the Tiffany Owens murder case. Someone needed to know that Eddie was more than likely within thirty miles of Austin.

CHAPTER 41
A NIGHT AT HOME

Pete and Danni had agreed to stay home and babysit with Elizabeth while Sal and Madison went out for a night on Sixth Street, downtown Austin. Because every night on Sixth Street was a rowdy party with live music, from blues to classic rock and country and western, they didn't expect them home until the wee hours of the morning.

Danni moved to the CD player and clicked it on. Dianna Krall's, "The Look of Love," began to play, soft and low. She'd just fed Elizabeth and placed her in the crib in the guest room. Conveniently, Jazzy had a two-bedroom guesthouse that she'd offered to Pete, Madison, and the baby. For the time that Madison and the baby spent in the main house, they'd prepared another area for little Elizabeth. Both the guesthouse and the guest room in the main house had cribs and baby monitors.

"Would you like a glass of wine now, gorgeous?"

"That sounds wonderful."

"It's almost sunset. Come out onto the patio with me while I grill our steaks. I'll bring your wine out."

"Thanks, Pete. I'll get the appetizers."

"I already have them. The salad's ready, potatoes, everything."

Danni sighed. "Where were you the first half of my life?"

A corner of Pete's mouth turned up in a lopsided grin. "It doesn't matter, darlin.' You weren't available anyway. What matters is right now, tomorrow, and the next day."

Danni smiled, her eyes met his, and she warmed.

Pete took her in his arms and murmured, "They won't be back until much later."

Danni laughed, low and sexy, "No one will disturb us."

"Dance?" Pete asked, taking her into his arms.

Moving together with him as the sun began to set, Danni felt the heat generated between them, as well as the intense magnetism that was always present when they were together. Cheek to cheek, heart to heart, he moved slightly as his lips met hers in a long kiss that intensified with each second. Her heartbeat sped up a notch, and her knees felt like melted butter.

In the background, Elizabeth's voice, making sweet baby noises, sounded over the baby monitor.

"A reminder, sweetheart, you check the baby and I'll check the steaks."

"Okay. If she's all right and just playing, we'd better enjoy our dinner while we can."

***

Danni sat down in a patio chair, took a sip of wine, and then a cracker with cheese smeared on it.

"We'll have a night off tomorrow. Would you like to go into town for dinner? Or would you rather take Jazzy up on her offer of taking her cruiser out on the lake for a private dinner, say around sunset?"

Danni chuckled. "The latter, of course. I can't think of anything more romantic than being alone with you at sunset on the lake."

"Neither can I."

"My divorce will be final soon. I keep wondering about

201

Vince, if he's dead or alive."

"Are you thinking that he might have had an accident, survived, but suffered from amnesia?"

"That, or maybe he had an accident and is in a coma in a hospital somewhere," Danni said.

"If you really believe that, then we should be checking the hospital records in Albuquerque and Santa Fe for admissions around the date of the crash."

"That may be something that was overlooked."

"It might be farfetched…then again, maybe not. What would you do if you were right?"

"Make sure he's receiving proper care. When he recovers, the first thing he needs to know is that he is a father. Secondly, that I've filed a Dissolution of Marriage. I'd also strongly suggest that he marry Madison," Danni said. "Elizabeth needs a father and Madison needs a husband."

Pete laughed. "Maybe we should stay out of her business. She might not want Vince now."

CHAPTER 42
UNFORTUNATE TIMING

After a delicious dinner at the one of the most famous restaurants in downtown Austin, Sal and Madison moved on to Jazzy's on 6th for her performance. When they entered the club, they were stunned by the crowd that she'd drawn. Her dynamite figure was clad in a long, sleek black skirt slit to the thigh, and a low-cut black top that hugged her narrow waist. Funky bracelets, earrings, and a belt to match complemented her outfit. Singing her heart out to the tune of "Mean to Me" in the old style of Billie Holiday, Jazzy mesmerized her audience. The piano player and saxophonist, both New Orleans transplants, were equally as good.

***

Thunder blasted, shaking the building, lightning flashed, and the rain fell in big drops. Eddie pulled into a parking space almost directly in front of Jazzy's. What were the chances of that? Must be his lucky night. He dashed into the club, barely getting wet. He surveyed the room and stopped. He couldn't believe his eyes. *What's Danni doing here, in Austin, in this club*? He moved through the crowd just close enough to watch her. Looking for a waitress, his eyes moved to his left. Damn! Sal was moving toward her with two glasses in his hands.

"Would you like a drink, sir?" the waitress standing next to Eddie asked.

"Just a beer. Whatever you have on draft. Oh, and send the singer a glass of wine or whatever her favorite drink is."

Eddie moved his eyes from Danni to Jazzy. Moving from "Mean to me," she picked up her pace with "Got My Mojo Workin'." Sexy little dance. He shook his head and the corners of his thin lips turned up. *Jazzy looks like Danni in some ways.* His eyes moved back to where Danni was sitting. Damn! He'd like to punch Sal senseless and carry Danni out of here and away to Giddings.

The waitress set the beer down on the table in front of Eddie. "Would you like to run a tab?"

"Oh, yeah. Say, where's the singer from? I think I've seen her before, but not in Austin."

"She moved here from New Orleans with some of the musicians in town after Hurricane Katrina."

He nodded and glanced up to her. "Thanks."

"Anytime," she said, the corners of her full lips turning up. "Just let me know if you need anything else."

"You can count on it, babe."

Another blast of thunder shook the building. The lights flickered.

Eddie took a pull of the draft, set it down, and glanced over to where Danni was sitting. She turned as though she knew he'd seen her. She wore a puzzled expression on her face, as if she didn't recognize him. Something wasn't right. Her hair didn't look the same, and she looked bigger. He shrugged his shoulders. She could have gained weight. His thin brows furrowed. He remembered something she'd told him over lunch at the house that she'd lived in on Highlands Beach, during a conversation about him being a foster child. He'd asked about her family.

Her reply had been that most of her family had been killed in a hurricane in Louisiana a few years ago...all but her aunt, who was a singer. She'd been out of town on a gig when Hurricane Katrina hit. Hell, this was Danni's aunt. He'd bet on it.

Eddie unhooked his cell phone and began to text Mark. *I need a background check on Danni Giardini, along with a list of her relatives. Check Austin for a singer by the name of Jazzy who plays at a club on Sixth Street. I'll try to find out her last name. Get back to me as soon as you can.*

He finished his beer and ordered another. Halfway through it, Sal rose, along with Danni. They were leaving. He couldn't let them get away. Eddie slammed some bills down on the table, enough to pay for the drinks and more. He rose and moved toward the door.

Sal and the woman stopped, turned, and moved toward Jazzy, who had finished her set, and stopped to talk with her. Eddie headed out of the club and moved to his car. He watched, climbed in, and waited. When they came out, he followed them from a distance. He smirked when he saw them climb into the sports car...a new Porsche. Another one to blow up.

***

Sal popped the umbrella open when they stepped outside of the club, took Madison's hand in his, and led her to the car.

"I thought I saw Pete come into the club," Madison said. "But then I realized it wasn't him, but someone else that looked very much like him. I knew it wasn't Pete as soon as I saw the scar on his nose."

Sal drew his heavy dark brows together. "That sounds like Eddie."

"Eddie? The man who kidnapped Danni?"

Sal nodded.

"He hasn't been caught yet?"

205

"No."

"You said that I resemble Danni. Pete told me that, too. I don't see it myself, except for the color and cut of our hair. I'm taller than, and not as slim as Danni."

"But from a distance you look alike. I didn't see him," Sal said. "I wish you would have mentioned it before."

"I'm sorry. You were picking up the drinks then, and I didn't see him again."

"That's all right, sweetie."

When they stepped into the Porsche, Sal turned on his cell phone. He clicked on messages, entered his password, and listened. "Damn!"

"What is it? It's not about the baby, is it?"

"No. It was Bobby calling from Florida. He remembered something that Eddie had told him a couple of months ago. His first set of foster parents lived on a ranch just outside of Austin. He thinks that with the police searching for him in Florida, he may be in Texas."

"And this guy looks like Pete?"

Sal heaved a sigh. "Yes."

"Then the man that I saw enter the club may have been Eddie."

"I think so."

"He thought that I was Danni. That's why he was staring."

CHAPTER 43
ACCIDENT!

Eddie's narrow mouth split into a wide grin. It wouldn't be long now and he'd have Danni back. This time he'd keep her in sight. Even though Mark hadn't texted him back yet, he knew it was her. Sal wouldn't be around to take her away from him again. He'd see to that. His car slid. Damn! The rain had begun to pick up. Roads were slick. Why didn't Sal slow down?

He sped up and crawled right up on his tail. When Sal turned onto Route 2222, he stayed with him. The Porsche's brake lights lit. Eddie braked and swerved toward the left so that he didn't plow into the Porsche. The car that Eddie was driving hydroplaned, and slid into a one-hundred-eighty degree turn, heading directly toward the edge of the cliff.

The car coming toward Eddie's braked and lost control. Sal jerked the wheel toward the right to avoid a head-on collision. Braking, he slid to the right, smashing into the side of the mountain.

CHAPTER 44
NOTIFICATION

Pete and Danni had fallen asleep on the huge sofa, entwined with each other. Soft instrumental music drifted from the music system. Elizabeth was sound asleep when Pete's cell phone rang.

"Hello. Yes. This is Pete Langley speaking."

Danni opened her eyes, sat up and, looked quizzically at Pete.

"We'll be there as soon as we can."

"What happened?"

"Aw, damn. There's been an accident on Route 2222 involving three cars. The drivers of two of the cars are dead. One of the cars went off the cliff. They believe the driver of that car was Eddie Haywood. Sal is in the emergency room, and Madison's in intensive care. The body of the man believed to be Eddie Haywood is in the morgue. They've called the registered owner of the vehicle, but haven't been able to reach him. You may need to identify his body."

Danni's hand flew to her heart. "Jesus, Lord!"

"Call Jazzy and ask her to come home after her last set so that she can watch Elizabeth."

"What time is it now?"

Pete glanced at his watch. "About one o'clock."

"She should be about finished. I'll call her at the club."

Pete moved to the window. It had stopped raining. The storm had moved on. Though the streets would be slick, it would be safe for Jazzy to drive home to Lakeway.

Danni clicked off her cell phone. "She's coming home just as soon as she finishes this set. She'll be on her way in about fifteen minutes."

"I'd rather her take her time than rush home on slick roads tonight."

Danni nodded. "Both Madison and Sal are receiving medical treatment and being carefully watched. The outcome is in the hands of God."

CHAPTER 45
THE MORGUE

"Doctor, I'm Pete Langley, Madison Langley's cousin, and this is Danni Giardini, Sal Catalano's friend and business partner. The last we heard, Mr. Catalano was in the emergency room and Miss Langley was in intensive care after suffering a terrible accident on Route 2222 a few hours ago."

The doctor nodded. "Yes. We've been waiting for you both. Mr. Catalano is in the emergency room being examined. His injuries were minor. Ms. Langley is in surgery. She suffered a concussion and a subdural hematoma."

Pete drew his brows together.

"We'll keep you posted in regard to both patients. The driver of the vehicle that went over the cliff didn't make it. When he was brought to the hospital, he was severely injured and just barely hanging onto life. He died within minutes of being brought into the emergency ward. We've tried to contact the owner of the vehicle, but haven't been able to yet. We found a wallet in the victim's pocket, and believe he was Mr. Eddie Haywood. There was a photograph of you in the wallet with your telephone number on the back of it, Ms. Giardini. Were you acquainted with him?"

Danni nodded. "He was an employee of JVS, at our Boca

Raton, Florida office."

"Would you be able to identify him?"

"Yes."

Pete stood and said, "Doctor, I've met Mr. Haywood. I'd like to go with you and Ms. Giardini to identify the body."

"Thanks, Pete. I could use the company."

"It will help to have a friend along." He took her hand in his and held it tight.

"Well then," the doctor said, "let's go to the morgue."

The morgue was close to the emergency room and the pathology department. A hearse approached, screened from the view of patients and public, and was just outside. She had the creeps from the moment she entered the room. The mortuary technician spoke to them and retrieved a body on a stretcher from a cold storage room. He unwrapped the shroud and pulled down the sheet.

"Oh, my God," Dannie said in a low tone of voice.

"Is this Eddie Haywood?"

Danni stood looking down at Eddie's remains. "As far as I can tell, that is the body of Eddie Haywood. He had cigarette burns on his left arm, and had recently cut his right arm. He had a tattoo of an eagle and a scorpion." She closed her eyes a moment then said, "His home was in Collier County, Florida, just a few miles west of Everglades City. He kept an apartment in Pompano Beach, Florida, too. As far as I know, he had foster brothers and sisters in Miami."

"Thank you, Ms. Giardini. I'm hoping the owner of the vehicle is one of his foster brothers. In the event that we can't locate him, would you, as his employer, be willing to claim his body?"

"Excuse me," Pete said. "That's way too much to ask of Ms. Giardini. She was recently abducted and held captive by this man. She only recently escaped. He's wanted for questioning on a murder charge in Florida, as well as on a charge of kidnapping Ms. Giardini. We have the name and telephone number of the officer in charge of the case. You might want to give him a call."

"Absolutely. I'm sorry to have put you through this, Ms. Giardini."

Danni nodded. "Apology accepted."

"May we go now?" Pete asked. "We would really like to see our friend, Sal. Please let us know when Madison Langley is out of surgery. I'm really worried about her. Several people in the past few years have died of concussions, specifically subdural hematomas."

"That's true," the doctor said. "But Ms. Langley has an advantage over those unfortunate victims. She has received immediate treatment. You and Ms. Giardini are free to go now."

When they returned to the waiting room, they sat down with others waiting for their loved ones. An old movie was playing on TV. One of the men waiting switched it to the Weather Channel. A category four hurricane was headed toward Florida, and was expected to strike the southeast coast between Ft. Lauderdale and the Jupiter Inlet by the following evening.

"Oh, my God! I can't believe it. I wonder if Bobby knows it's coming."

"I expect he does. Surfers usually know exactly what's going on with the weather. But you might want to give him a call. That's a hell of a big storm. He'll need to close up all of the hurricane shutters, do what he can to protect the property, and get out of there."

Danni clicked on her cell and called Bobby. No one answered. She left a message and asked him to call her as soon as he could.

"If I hadn't escaped from Eddie's home in the glades, I'd be stuck there during the storm."

"Maybe. Held hostage by Eddie's friend, Mark, and his buddies, the rapist and drug dealers, you might not have lived that long."

Danni paled. "That's right. I might not have."

"You were lucky."

"Ms. Giardini?" The doctor approached.

"Yes."

"Mr. Catalano had been treated for his injuries and is ready to go home now."

"Wonderful."

Pete drew his brows together and cleared his throat. "Doctor, has Madison Langley come out of surgery yet?"

"Yes. She has. Everything went well and she's in the recovery room. You may wait and see her if you like."

"We will definitely be waiting, and I'm sure that Mr. Catalano will want to see her before he goes home, too."

Danni punched in Jazzy's cell phone number. "Hey! I knew you would be wondering about Sal and Madison. Sal's going to be just fine. He's been treated for minor injuries that he suffered in the accident. Madison's just come out of surgery. Evidently, she's going to be all right, too, but we will need to help her with Elizabeth while she recovers."

When she ended her conversation she turned to Pete and said, "Jazzy's happy to hear that both Sal and Madison are going to be fine. Bobby called and will be arriving in the morning with a friend. They will be renting a car, so we won't need to pick them up. When I asked her who the friend was and where they were staying, she said that she had made reservations for Bobby's friend at The Lakeway Inn."

"I wonder who it is," Pete said. "I didn't know Bobby had a girlfriend."

"Neither did I."

"Mr. Langley, you may see your cousin now. She's been transferred from the recovery room to a private room. Ms. Giardini, Mr. Catalano will be coming out in a wheelchair soon. We require that he stay in the wheelchair while he's here. We'll bring him out to your car when you're ready to leave. I'm assuming that you and Mr. Catalano will be waiting for Mr. Langley to return."

"Yes, of course."

"Please let us know when you are ready to leave."

CHAPTER 46
SURPRISE VISITOR

Danni awoke to the aroma of rich coffee brewing and bacon frying. She padded into the bathroom, took a quick shower, and dressed in a pair of jeans and a lemon yellow scoop designer tee. After she'd brushed her hair, she spent a few moments applying blush, lip-gloss, eye shadow, liner, and mascara. Slipping into a pair of heels, she followed the delicious scents to the breakfast room, which overlooked Lake Travis.

"Oh my God!"

The color in Danni's face drained. She reached for the table to steady herself. Closing her eyes, she struggled to compose herself. Her mind was whirling, her stomach churning. She thought that she was going to be ill.

"Are you all right?"

She gasped. It was his voice. She hadn't imagined him sitting there in front of her. She opened her eyes.

"Sweet Jesus! You frightened me. I thought you were dead, or in a hospital somewhere." Danni sat in the chair opposite Vince. "Why didn't you give me some warning?"

"Didn't anyone tell you that I was here?"

"No. No one told me that you were still alive, either. All of us thought you had been killed in the airline crash."

"By the grace of God, I wasn't."

Bobby walked into the breakfast room with two cups of coffee, one for Danni and one for himself. He set a cup down in front of her. "You didn't know?"

Danni shook her head.

"I'm sorry. I thought Jazzy would have told you that I was bringing Uncle Vince. I almost had a heart attack myself when he walked into the JVS Sales Office a few days ago. I hope someone has told Sal."

"I doubt anyone has. It was late when we came in last night, and Sal had already been through a lot. I'm sure he went right to sleep. As far as I know, he's still sleeping." Danni glanced at Vince. "You must be who Jazzy referred to as Bobby's friend."

"Evidently. At any rate, I'm happy to be referred to as someone's friend, especially after I betrayed you, deserted Sal and Bobby, and disappeared from Madison's life."

Danni snorted. "I'll say. You've got a lot of explaining to do to a lot of people. First of all, you should probably know that I have filed for a Dissolution of Marriage. Since I didn't know where you were or if you had survived the airline crash, I published a notification in the Palm Beach Post. Alive or not, you could hardly expect me to stay married to you after I discovered that you had a mistress."

"Bobby filled me in on a few things before we flew out of Orlando. I hope that we can stay friends. I realize that I hurt you. I'm sorry. How can I ever make it up to you?"

"You can't, but thank you for your apology, Vince. There's nothing more that you can do. Our marriage began to head south a few years ago. I've already forgiven you for your affair with Madison." She smirked. "The fact that you didn't tell her that you were married was a poor choice, but that's something Madison needs to forgive you for, not me."

"I expect I'm in the doghouse."

She shrugged her shoulders. "I'm just glad that you weren't on the flight that crashed. It's been over six months since that happened. Where have you been?"

"Unconscious and in a coma for the most part."

She nodded.

"I'll wait and finish my story when Sal's ready for breakfast. I hear he and Madison had a bad accident last night."

Danni closed her eyes and sighed. "Horrendous. Several people died. Madison's lucky that she wasn't killed. She's a wonderful girl, and it would have been a tragedy if she'd died."

"Is she all right?" Vince asked, his brows furrowing.

"She will be."

"Good. How did you meet her?"

Danni laughed. "Later. We have a lot of stories to tell you, Vince."

Pete entered the breakfast room. "I smell coffee. Is there any left?"

"Sit down, Pete." Danni rose from her chair. "I'll get it. Refill anyone?"

Vince glanced at Pete with a curious expression upon his face. "Haven't I met you?"

Pete did a double take. "My God! Back from the dead? It's Vince, isn't it?"

Vince nodded.

Danni set Pete's cup of coffee down in front of him. "Pete, this is Vince Giardini. Vince, this is Pete Langley, my very good friend, and Madison's cousin."

"We've met."

"I didn't know you were acquainted with Danni and everyone else here," Vince said.

Pete glanced at Danni, a sparkle in his amber eyes and a

mischievous grin on his face. "Has he met Elizabeth?"

"No." Danni chuckled.

"I'll check in on her. She may want to join the crowd."

Pete rose from his seat at the table and returned about ten minutes later with Elizabeth in his arms and a bottle of formula.

"Vince, this is the newest member of our family, Elizabeth Victoria Langley."

Vince grinned widely. "She's beautiful."

The corners of Danni's lips turned up into a gentle smile. "She's just two months old. Adorable, isn't she? We all love her."

The color drained from Vince's face.

"She looks a lot like you, Uncle Vince."

"Especially the coloring," Danni said. "And her ears."

Elizabeth focused her eyes upon Vince and made little baby noises.

"Would you like to hold her?" Pete asked. "She'll be hungry soon, but I brought a bottle of formula with me. I've already warmed it."

Pete rose, moved to Vince, and placed Elizabeth in his arms.

Vince smiled, gazing down at the baby. "Who does she belong to?"

"She's yours and Madison's. Her name should officially be Elizabeth Victoria Langley Giardini."

Vince choked. "I had no idea. My God. Madison had this baby all by herself."

"I was there while she was pregnant, Vince," Pete said. "So was her friend Jeannie, and later, your partner, Sal."

"Sal! What was Sal doing there?"

"When Sal and Danni discovered that you had a mistress, he called on Madison," Pete said. "Someone had to tell her that you had been in a plane crash; that you were thought to have been killed in the accident."

"That must have been a shock to everyone."

"It was," Danni said.

"Thank you, all of you, for helping Madison through this. At some point, Danni, you must have befriended Madison."

"Yes. I did. She didn't know that you were a married man when she began her affair with you. Why would I be angry with her? Besides, she is one of my best friends' cousins."

"So, all of you have become good friends."

Danni and Pete nodded.

Vince glanced down at Elizabeth. "She's adorable; the sweetest little baby I've ever seen. If Madison agrees, I would like her to be christened Elizabeth Victoria Langley Giardini."

"She may agree to that," Pete said, "but I'm not sure that she would marry you. Madison's a sensitive woman, and she has a lot to learn about forgiveness. In fact, you have a lot of nerve showing up here without any warning. Did you even consider how Danni would feel? Or Madison?"

Vince drew his brows together. "I had no way of knowing."

"I coaxed him into coming with me," Bobby said. "We didn't have much time to discuss it with the hurricane coming."

"No," Pete said. "I suppose you didn't."

"Excuse me. I need to help Jazzy." Danni rose from the chair that she had been sitting on.

Jazzy and Danni carried in platters of fruit, scrambled eggs, bacon, homemade-hashed browns, and English muffins. They had set the table for five, but realized that they needed one more place setting. When they went back into the room, Sal was sitting across from Vince. He wore an expression that told everyone who saw him that he was the happiest man in the world in spite of his bruises.

"Man! I've never been so surprised in my life!"

"We were all surprised."

"I'm glad to have my partner back. I wasn't sure what I was going to do. I was hoping that Pete would join us."

"If you really need me, I'll help you," Pete said. "But I'd like to stick to my current lines of work."

"I figured that."

"Will you tell us about how you came to miss your flight?" Jazzy asked. "I know we're all very interested in hearing your story."

Vince took a bite of scrambled eggs, then a sip of coffee. "Sure. I realized when I left the plane to retrieve my backpack that I had a choice. The ride from LAX to Albuquerque had been hell. I had a gut feeling that the flight was headed toward disaster. The fact that they hadn't made the mechanical repairs needed and intended to continue on to Denver alarmed me. Once I'd left the plane, I felt relieved and didn't reboard. I figured that, if the plane arrived in Denver safely, either Thomas or Sal would retrieve my luggage or it would be sent on to the chalet where we planned to stay in Aspen." He paused and took another bite of scrambled eggs and a slice of bacon.

"Why didn't you call me, Vince?" Sal asked.

Vince sighed deeply. "I tried once or twice to get through, but kept receiving the message that 'all circuits are busy.' I thought it might be due to weather interference, and planned to call again later once I was on the shuttle to Taos."

"Taos?" Danni asked. "Why Taos?"

"You do remember that I have a friend there who is a developer in northern New Mexico and Colorado, don't you? I figured I'd stop by, say hello, rent a car, and continue on to Aspen from there. I was in no mood to board another flight. It was no problem booking the shuttle and a room at the Taos Inn. I tried again to reach Sal about halfway to Taos, but I received the same message. After that, it was too late. The weather was inclement, the pass into Taos treacherous. The driver hit an icy patch and lost control of the shuttle. We slid off the road and over the cliff. That's all I remember. I was in a coma for months. Evidently, I was airlifted to St. Vincent's Hospital in Santa Fe."

"Huh," Sal said. "I should have thought of that."

"I could have sworn you visited me in a dream, Uncle Vince. It was about a week after you left. I dreamed that you came to visit me; that you said you were all right and it was nice where you were. I thought you were dead."

"In some ways I was. No one really knows where the mind goes, or if you can hear people talking when you're in a coma. But I'll tell you, my spirit must have traveled. I remember visiting you, Bobby. Right after I blacked out or went into the coma, I saw a beautiful meadow. While I was unconscious, I heard people speaking to me…nurses, doctors, and a couple of people from Taos, including a young woman by the name of Margarite who visited me weekly. Don't ever think that patients who are comatose can't hear what's said around them."

Danni buttered her English muffin and smeared strawberry jam on it. Taking a bite, then a sip of coffee, she lightly blotted her mouth. "There were several times that I felt you were with me, in spirit. That was one of the major factors that convinced me that you had died. That, and the watch that was found in the wreckage. Otherwise, I would have said you would never have continued on to Denver in a plane with mechanical problems."

"What about the watch?"

"The airline officials found a charred watch with the initials VG on the back of it."

"I was in a hurry to leave from our resort in Mexico to the Puerto Vallarta International Airport. Rather than take the time to pack it in my carry on, I slipped the watch into the pocket of my windbreaker. Later, I packed the jacket in my suitcase, not thinking about the watch. I'd just purchased a watch in Mexico and was wearing that one…the one that I'm wearing now." He rolled the cuff of his shirtsleeve up. "Like it? The watch band is Mexican silver from Taxco."

"It's beautiful, Vince," Danni said.

"I didn't know that you were going to Mexico," Sal said. "Why didn't you tell me?"

"It was a last minute decision. I wanted to check some things out at the resort; see if it needs any repairs or additions."

Sal nodded. "That was a good idea. We'll talk about that later though. Go on with your story."

"Anyway, I took my parka on the plane with me since I knew it was going to be cold when I arrived in Denver. Before I left LAX, I stuffed the windbreaker in the luggage that I later checked in."

"So, when the plane crashed, your windbreaker, with your old watch in the pocket, was in the luggage that was stowed in the baggage area of the plane."

"Right."

"Well," Danni said, "that explains it. We thought you always wore the watch."

"I did, until I bought this one."

CHAPTER 47
DANNI'S STORY

After they finished breakfast, Danni told her story about Eddie. She and Pete both told about how they had become friends. Neither disclosed the fact that they had formed a strong bond, and that their attraction was equally as strong.

"Why Austin? Why are all of you here?" Vince asked. "Was it because I briefly spoke with you about the real estate market in Texas still being active?"

"Partially. Most of all, I believed that Danni's life was in danger and that she needed to leave Florida for a while. Jazzy's here, and Danni wanted to visit."

"Unfortunately," Pete said, "By the time we arrived in Austin, the same danger that she had faced in Florida was waiting for her here. The only thing that stopped Eddie from kidnapping her again or killing her was the accident that Sal and Madison had last night. Eddie had seen them at Jazzy's on 6th and had mistaken Madison for Danni. From a distance they bear a resemblance to each other."

"They do, don't they?" Vince commented.

"Unfortunately for Madison, yes."

"Have you had time to check out the development potential here?"

"We think, as far as homes, it may be too late," Sal said. "There are other areas of development that need to be considered. Lakeway and Westlake could use a couple of nice hotels, more upscale restaurants that provide live entertainment. The majority of people in Lakeway don't want to travel into Austin to hear live entertainment, plus there's a demand for something more upscale than Sixth Street provides. Lakeway has an older crowd."

"I haven't seen an art gallery either," Pete said. "There must be a demand for galleries with all of the beautiful homes. I'm sure there must be artists here. Where do they display their work?"

"That's a good question. Where do the owners of these multi-million dollar homes purchase their antiques and original paintings?"

"I don't know, but these are areas that need to be considered," Vince said. "Let's check it out, Sal."

"Would you like to look around later this afternoon?"

"Hell yes," Vince said. "That is, if you're up to it after your accident, and if Pete and Danni don't mind taking care of Elizabeth this afternoon. I'm guessing that Madison won't be up to seeing visitors for a while. Are you sure she's okay? That they will let us see her? Subdural hematoma patients sometimes fall into a coma after or during surgery."

"She was placed in intensive care after the accident last night, and had surgery almost immediately," Pete said. "I saw her after she was transferred to her room from recovery. She was still out of it and looked very pale. I'm planning to visit later this morning, if she is allowed visitors. I expect you would like to come along."

"I would, but she doesn't need a shock. She thinks I'm dead."

Danni cleared her throat. "I think it would be best if you give Madison a couple of days to recover. She almost died."

"But, she might want to see Vince," Pete said. "I've known Madison all of my life. She'll be furious with all of us if she thinks we lied to her or concealed Vince's presence from her. Why don't you ride along to the hospital with me? If I think she is up to it, I'll explain that you're with us now. Then you can see her."

"Elizabeth will be fine with us."

Vince's eyes lit with anticipation. "I'd really like to see her. I never meant to leave her in the position that she found herself."

CHAPTER 48
MADISON

Pete and Vince drove over Route 2222 on their way to the hospital that Madison had been airlifted to.

"My God!" Vince said when he saw where Eddie Haywood had gone off the cliff. "No wonder he was killed. I don't remember meeting him."

"I understand that after your memorial service, the original gardener quit. Not long after that, Eddie showed up at your front door looking for a job as a gardener. Danni was so upset after the memorial service that she didn't take a full application. She had two references, but couldn't reach either."

"Why did she hire him then?"

"Eddie had charisma and was good at what he did. As far as appearances go, we resembled each other, at least from a distance. Danni said that women loved him." Pete shook his head. "Too bad. He was a monster."

"I'm sure glad that you met Danni. He very well might have killed her."

"Yeah, he probably would have, In fact, he almost killed Sal and Madison."

"The bastard."

"We believe that he had a mental illness; borderline

personality disorder."

"So," Vince said, "he probably wasn't on medication and wasn't receiving therapy."

"That's exactly right."

"Similar to my deceased partner, who was also mentally ill."

"I expect so."

"I'll sure be glad to see Madison. How do you think she feels about me? She shouldn't be raising Elizabeth alone," Vince said. "Do you think she might accept a proposal of marriage?"

"I can't speak for Madison, but I'll tell you that she was quite upset when she discovered you were married. Danni's been wonderful. Not many women would forgive her husband's mistress, but she did."

"I have a lot to make up for to both Danni and to Madison."

"I can't argue with that."

"I'm curious. How close are you and Danni? It looks to me like you're a lot more than friends."

Pete sighed. "To tell you the truth, Vince, I'm really taken with Danni. Once the divorce is over, which should be soon, I intend to let her know how I feel about her."

"I suspected that was the case. That's fine, Pete. I just think it's odd the way things worked out."

"Me too. I literally bumped into Danni in Palm Beach. She was going to pick up a painting in one of the galleries that my oil paintings are displayed in."

"Interesting. I met Madison in her bookstore in Tequesta, and I rarely go into bookstores. Danni was ill. I had other business in the shopping center. When I saw the bookstore, I stopped in and bought a suspense novel for Danni. When I first set eyes on Madison, I knew right away that I was a goner."

Pete laughed. "Love at first sight. Destiny, I'd call it."

"The only reason that Danni and I were still together was

because of our religion. I should say my religion, because Danni converted because of me. I don't know where she goes to church now."

"Danni, Bobby, and I go to church with Jazzy. It's a non-denominational Christian church. Sal attends the Catholic Church in Lakeway."

"Well, there are many paths. All lead to the same direction, and it's great if you find the one that calls to you."

Pete nodded. "We're almost there. Do you want to sit in the waiting room for a few minutes while I prepare Madison for the ultimate surprise?"

"Please. I don't want to give her a heart attack. Besides, it will give me time to watch the news. I need to know where the hurricane struck."

***

For the first time, Pete didn't need to wait to see Madison. When he arrived at her room, he opened the door just a crack to peek in so that he wouldn't disturb her if she were sleeping.

"Hey Pete. Come in and keep me company."

"Wow! I'm sure glad to see you up and doing so well."

"Do you know what they did to me?"

"I spoke with your doctor. From what I understand, you had a sub-acute subdural hematoma due to a head injury from the accident. This type of subdural hematoma usually has a favorable outcome once the blood collection has been drained. The symptoms go away in most cases."

"I feel much better. I don't have a headache."

"You're speaking well."

"Thank the good Lord."

"How's your memory?"

"Okay, I think."

"Good," Pete said. "Memory loss is cited as a possible

complication that follows a subdural hematoma. I need to ask you an important question."

"Okay."

"Do you remember Vince?"

Her lips turned up at the corners and she chuckled. "What a question! Of course, I remember Vince. He was my daughter's father."

"If I told you that he survived the accident, would you want to see him?"

Madison's face lit up. Her eyes sparkled. "Are you telling me that Vince is alive; that somehow or other he escaped the accident alive?"

The corners of Pete's mouth turned up. "Yes. That's what I'm telling you."

"Is he here?"

Pete nodded.

"At the hospital?"

"He's in the waiting room."

"What's he doing out there? Tell him to come in."

***

After escorting Vince to Madison's room, Pete returned to the waiting room to allow them their privacy. Vince had much to tell her and to apologize for. He wasn't sure if she would still want him. It seemed as though Madison and Sal had become very good friends.

Pete reached over for the TV changer and clicked the station to the Weather Channel. "A category four hurricane zeroed in on Hollywood, Florida last night. Power is out all along the coast; the National Guard has been called in and FEMA is on its way. Lootings are occurring everywhere. Water is contaminated; roads are flooded. Watch out for fallen power lines. Animals have escaped the zoos and alligators are everywhere. The damage is unbelievable from Miami to Stuart, Florida. If you evacuated for the hurricane, stay where you are until you are told that you may come back."

"Jeez." He pulled out his cell phone and punched in Sal's number. "Hey. Have you watched the news? Turn on the Weather Channel. We'll talk about the storm when we're back at Jazzy's. Madison looks good. I don't think they will keep her long."

CHAPTER 49
A NEW BEGINNING

Madison had been home a week and was continuing to improve. Six weeks later, Vince asked Pete and Danni if they would watch Elizabeth for the evening while he took Madison out to dinner.

"So," Danni said, her lips turning up at the corners, "you're finally going to do the right thing."

Vince sighed. "If she will have me."

"For Elizabeth's sake, I hope she will."

"Personally, I think she could do better," Pete said. "If she agrees, you had better not ever cheat on her or you will be answering to me, and Madison's father as well. Both of us are bigger than you."

"I'll keep that in mind."

***

Madison was admiring the fabulous view of Lake Travis while sipping a glass of champagne with Vince. It was her first outing since the accident. The lake was calm, reflecting the full moon's light. Hill country deer grazed nearby.

"You look beautiful tonight, Madison."

"Thank you. I feel beautiful sitting here on the terrace in the midst of all of this beauty."

"Do you remember the day we met?"

"It was almost two years ago, wasn't it?"

"To the day. For me, it was love at first sight. Every time I saw you from then on, I could barely control myself."

"It's just too bad that our timing was off and you were still married to Danni."

"Our divorce is final now, and I'm thankful that Danni and I are still friends."

"You should be. Most people wouldn't have been that forgiving."

"I don't know how I can make it up to either of you."

"Just be honest to everyone, no matter the cost," Madison said. "Everyone makes mistakes sometimes."

"I'll make it a point never to do anything that will hurt anyone else, no matter the temptation," Vince said.

"Those are two points our daughter needs to learn at an early age."

"And she will. To change the subject, do you like Austin, Lakeway in particular?"

"I do. I love the lake, the topography, and the friendly people. I never expected to see palm trees and bougainvillea here."

"The first time I visited Austin, the area was a surprise to me, too. Would you like to live here, near the lake, during Florida's stormy season?"

"I can't say yet. I've only been here a short time, and I've just gone through a terrible experience. Why do you ask?"

"I've been seriously thinking of purchasing a home here. In fact, I have chosen one not far from here with a fabulous view of the lake. I'd like you to see it."

"Why? It will be your home. You don't need my approval."

"Actually I do. I'm hoping that you and Elizabeth will live there with me."

"What?"

Vince took a small silver box from his jacket pocket and placed it on the table in front of her.

"Is this an anniversary gift in remembrance of our meeting two years ago?"

"Not exactly. I'm hoping that you will say yes to a fall wedding. Marry me, Madison." Vince opened the small box, removed the four-carat diamond ring, and slipped it onto the third finger of her left hand.

Madison's hand flew to cover her heart. "Oh! I never expected this."

"I love you Madison. I want to spend the rest of my life with you and our child."

"I don't know what to say."

"Say yes."

She shook her head. "I'm not ready for this, Vince. A year and a half ago, I would have said yes in a heartbeat. But that was before I knew that you had betrayed Danni and lied to me."

Vince rubbed his forehead. "I'm sorry. I've apologized to both of you. What can I do to convince you that I will never lie or cheat on anyone again?"

"I don't know. I haven't forgotten how I felt when I discovered that you were married, or how I felt being a single mother when Elizabeth was born. It was Sal and Jeannie who helped me through the pregnancy and the birth. I know that wasn't your fault. You were lying in a hospital in a coma." Madison removed the ring from her finger and handed it back to Vince. "I'm sorry. The ring is beautiful, but I just can't accept your proposal right now."

"I should have known better. I rushed you. You must know that I would never have allowed you to go through childbirth alone. But since I couldn't be there, you were lucky to have Sal around."

"I was."

"Unless you tell me that you don't want to see me, I promise you that I intend to change your mind about marrying me."

"I do want to you in my life, Vince, and I want our daughter to know you and that you are her father."

"Keep the ring, Madison. Wear it and enjoy it."

"It wouldn't be right to keep your ring or even wear it, not at this point. I would feel obligated to you. You've been gone a long time. I thought you were dead; that you weren't coming back. Don't misunderstand...I'm so glad that you were not on the plane that crashed, that you are alive and well. But, I'm a different person now. I'm a mother. I've met new people, changed my philosophy about many things. As a plus to you," she added, her mouth curving up into a beautiful smile, "I'm much more forgiving."

"Thank God. Those are all positive things, Madison. I think I love you even more now. Are you saying that we need to become reacquainted? I've changed too, you know. I was in a coma for months after hovering on the edge of death. After experiencing that, my philosophies have changed drastically."

"That's the point, Vince. We're no longer the same people that we were two years ago. We need to get to know each other all over again."

"Have you met someone else?"

"I'm not involved with anyone else, and I haven't been."

"How do you feel about Sal?"

"At this point, he's a good friend, and I don't know what I would have done without him."

"And that's all?"

"Sal's a nice looking man. I'd be lying if I said that I wasn't attracted to him."

"Hmm. It sounds like I may have competition. That just makes it more interesting," Vince said, sitting back with a smile on his face and a twinkle in his hazel eyes.

"You don't give up easily, do you?"

"No. If it takes me forever, I'm going to convince you that I am sincere; that I will be a loyal and faithful husband to you, and a good father to Elizabeth."

CHAPTER 50
RETURN TO FLORIDA

Pete, Danni, and Bobby departed Lakeway in JVS's private plane bound for Ft. Lauderdale International Airport. When they arrived, the pilot drove them to one of JVS's model homes near Glades Road and Interstate 95. Danni and Sal had generously given Bobby the model before Vince had arrived from New Mexico. When they advised him of their decision, Vince promptly agreed, especially since Bobby was an owner of the company as well.

"We're home, guys," Bobby said. "How do you like it? Sal's going to be sharing this with me until he finds something else. But, this is all mine, furniture and everything. Well, not exactly mine. It's titled under the corporation."

"As most everything is," Danni said. "It's better that way."

"It's a great house," Pete said. "I remember my first bachelor pad. It wasn't nearly as nice as this." He moved to the patio and gazed out. "Wow! A pool, too."

"Everything's perfect. You have an office, three bedrooms, two baths, a family room, living room, dining room, and a huge Florida room. I think you will enjoy it, and I hope that you like the furniture," Danni said, moving through the home. "You are so lucky that the home withstood the hurricane."

"I am, but as you can see," Bobby said, "the landscape all needs to be replaced. There's debris everywhere, and the pool screens were all ripped off during the storm."

"That's minimal damage," Danni said. "The important thing is, the roof is still on and the house is still standing." She glanced to Pete and said, "We build all of our homes to withstand hurricane force winds. Each of our homes has safe rooms. JVS's homes in Sarasota are built in the same manner."

"Good thing you called your manager here in Boca Raton before we left Austin," Pete said. "I never expected to see this kind of damage here. I thought the hurricane would drop down to a category three or even a high two, and strike Miami or the Keys."

"I couldn't believe it when the office manager called," Danni said. "The hurricane was a catastrophe for Dade, Broward, and Palm Beach Counties. The front of Sal's penthouse, which faced the Atlantic, was completely sheared off by the hurricane's winds. Every window was blown out; balconies no longer exist."

"Did he check Madison's home?" Pete asked, drawing his brows together.

"Yeah," Bobby said. "All that remains is a slab."

"Oh, man!"

"The good thing is that Vince and I were able to store the vehicles and the cabin cruiser. We removed paintings, art treasures, and photo albums from Sal and Madison's homes. Vince grabbed armloads of Sal's clothing. I have your better clothing, and most of Madison's and Pete's. As for me, I only had time to grab a few clothes and my favorite surfboards. My car, along with Pete's, is in the garage here."

Pete chuckled. "I'm sure glad a tree didn't fall on the garage."

"There's a lot to do besides contacting the insurance companies and FEMA," Pete said. "Are you sure you don't want

Danni and me to stay and help you?"

"Actually, now that I see the destruction, I would really appreciate it if you could stay until Sal arrives next week."

"Sure. We can do that," Pete said. "In fact, I'm going to need to deal with Madison's home and maybe her business, too, before I drive back over to the other coast."

"I didn't think about the bookstore. I'll help you with that, Pete," Danni said. "Bobby, would you contact Vince and Sal? Set up a conference call for later today. Include Pete and me in on it. They need to be aware of the extent of the damages here. We won't really know the total damage to JVS's homes until we've had time to assess them."

***

Sal arrived the next day. After viewing the near-total destruction to his penthouse, he sighed and ran his hand through his thick, dark hair. "Damn. First, my Porsche goes up in flames; next Danni's kidnapped; now a hurricane destroys my penthouse. What's going on here?"

"You need some good juju." Danni chuckled. "I'm not faring much better. First, my husband cheats on me, then he's killed, or so I think; then I'm kidnapped. But on the good side, I didn't die. I met both Pete and Madison, who have become wonderful friends, and I escaped a virtual madman."

"On the good side for me," Sal said, "is that I met Madison and Pete, my partner returned from the dead, and no one that I love died!"

"That's what counts," Pete said. "You can forget the material stuff."

CHAPTER 51
PRIVATE INTERLUDE

"I am so happy to be away from the destruction," Danni said with a deep sigh. "That was a mess...depressing, too. At least Madison's bookstore wasn't a complete disaster."

"For one, the construction is concrete, the shopping center is fairly new, so it had the new roofs designed to withstand hurricanes, and it isn't directly on the water."

"Madison may not be returning soon," Danni said, "so I'll be able to have it in good shape and looking great by the time she returns."

"If she does."

"Hmm. With my permission, along with Bobby and Vince's, Sal has chosen and reserved a home for her and Elizabeth in the same development as Bobby's. No strings attached. The title, if she returns, will be free and clear in her name."

"Wow! How generous of all of you."

"Madison deserves it. If the company hadn't agreed, Sal would have done it anyway. Maybe even Vince."

Pete grinned. "Sal's a good man."

"Vince made a poor decision, but basically he's a good guy, too," Danni said. "Tough in business though."

"I'll bet," Pete said.

"Madison's free to make her own decision now without being pressured by anyone. She doesn't need to accept the mansion that Vince has offered," Pete said, unlocking the front door of his small condo and studio in Fisherman's Cove.

Danni chuckled. "She hasn't accepted that rock that he offered her either."

"And she turned down his proposal," Pete said. "Madison's a strong woman and doesn't appreciate being lied to."

"If Vince can convince her that he will be a good father and be faithful to her, she may still accept his offer."

"She may," Pete said.

***

Pete pushed open the door and set the suitcases down inside. He turned to Danni and flashed her a rakish smile. "You did want to come to my place here on the water first, didn't you, gorgeous?"

Her mouth tipped up at the corners. "Oh God, yes."

"No one knows the telephone number here. My cell phone's off."

"Total privacy," Danni added, and clicked her cell phone off.

Pete swept Danni up into his arms and kicked the front door shut. "I've been waiting to be alone with you for a long, long time," he said, carrying her into the bedroom.

Her gaze met his sensual amber eyes. Her heartbeat quickened and she felt a tingling in the pit of her stomach. She unbuttoned the top button of his shirt, then the second and third.

Setting her down near the king-sized bed, his lips met hers and her world spun out of control. All thoughts other than becoming one with Pete fled from her mind. Unbuckling his belt, she unsnapped his jeans and pushed them down. The air surrounding them electrified her as he pulled her tank top off. Her breath quickened as the remains of their clothing pooled to

240

the floor.

When he pushed her down on the bed, a strong surge of desire ran through her. Her pulse beat erratically as she felt his body, strong and warm, cover hers. Their eyes locked and her cheeks warmed as he gazed down upon her. His kisses moving from her earlobe, down her long, slender neck, and onto her shoulders thrilled her. Winding her arms around him, she surrendered to their passion. By sunset, they were exhausted from their hours of lovemaking.

***

"Famished, darlin'?"

"Absolutely."

"I don't have much here. Would you be up to going to dinner on the Circle?"

"I'll be ready in about forty minutes."

"You shower and dress first. There's shampoo and conditioner in the shower, and a blow-dryer under the sink."

"Thanks, Pete."

"Sure. I'll bring the suitcases into the bedroom, then wait in the Florida room while you shower."

***

She sighed, turned on the shower, and stepped into the hot stream of water. Allowing it to flow over her and relax her muscles, she began to lather her hair. The scent from Pete's shampoo was exotic, sensual, and intoxicating. When she began to lather her skin with the soap, she found the scent the same. She wondered where he'd found the products. Did Madison use something similar? If so, Vince hadn't had a chance in the world.

***

After Pete brought the suitcases into the bedroom, he took a beer from the fridge, chips from the cabinet, and moved into the Florida room. Clicking on his cell phone, he scrolled through the messages.

"Hi, Pete, this is Madison. Sorry I missed you. I know you and Danni must be happy to have time to yourselves. It's getting cold here and I'm coming home. I'll be arriving in Ft. Lauderdale with Elizabeth tomorrow. Sal is picking us up from the airport. I'll call after I'm settled into the home in Boca tomorrow night or the next day. Love you."

Pete chuckled and his mouth split into a wide grin.

"Hey, looks like something has made you very happy."

Pete turned and cast an admiring glance and lopsided smile toward Danni.

She stood at the entrance of the Florida room, dressed in a sexy black sundress, high-heeled gold sandals, and gold dangling earrings, with a wide gold and pearl bracelet on her left wrist.

"You look luscious, darlin'."

Danni's lips turned up at the corners. "Thank you. Now, tell me the good news."

"First of all, that I'm here, alone with you. Secondly, Madison's flying into the Ft. Lauderdale airport tomorrow with Elizabeth. They will be living in the home that JVS offered them."

"Wonderful."

CHAPTER 52
PROGRESS IN AUSTIN

Vince had just dropped Madison and Elizabeth off at the airport. He already missed them, and wished that she hadn't decided to return to Florida so soon, though he suspected it was for her own and Elizabeth's health that she had done so. Madison had never liked cold weather, and although Austin winters were relatively mild, she feared that the baby would have colds all winter long. Vince promised Madison that he would visit both of them once every month for a weekend, at least. She still had not accepted his proposal, but he hoped that by springtime she would.

With permission from Sal, Danni, and Bobby, Vince began to plan expansion in the Austin area. He'd purchased the huge home overlooking Lake Travis. Since he still wasn't sure if Madison would accept his proposal of marriage, the home was categorized as JVS's Texas headquarters. Madison seemed to relax after that. If she chose to marry him, he would build one to suit both of their specifications.

Vince had also purchased several acres in Westlake, as well as in Bee Caves for the development of two resorts. In Lakeway he had drawn up plans for the development of a small, unique upscale shopping area that would feature small European,

French, and Mediterranean restaurants, as well as boutiques and several art galleries.

What he needed now was another hand to run the operation. He needed Sal, or Bobby. Danni had proven to be an excellent partner, but he didn't think that either she or Pete would agree to move to Austin. There was no doubt in his mind that she would not consider coming to Austin without Pete, not even for a weekend. He decided to place a conference call this afternoon.

***

"Sal, Bobby, Danni, this is Vince. I have everything together now and have hired a secretary who will also be able to handle the bookkeeping. It's Margarite Garcia, the young woman I met while I was in the hospital in Santa Fe. She's capable of handling both jobs, and has excellent references. Her father, Joseph, has also moved to Austin. He's in his mid-fifties and would like to work as our office manager. I know him well. He's an honest man and works hard."

"That sounds great!" Sal said.

"Danni, what do you think?"

"You're an excellent judge of people. If you're satisfied with them, so am I."

"Bobby?"

"Hey, Uncle Vin. Margarite and her father sound okay to me."

"Great. There's one more thing I need."

"What's that?" Sal asked. "You've saved it for last, so it must be important."

"It is. I need one of you to help me here."

The line went silent.

"That's what I was afraid of. Bobby, could you come out during the summer until you start school again?"

"Sure, Uncle Vince."

"Great! But I still need someone to help me during the year."

"I don't think any of us want to be in Austin during the winter months," Danni said.

"It's Pete. I'm here with Danni. I know that you didn't intend to include me in this call."

"I'm glad you're on the line, Pete. I appreciate your input with finances, as well as the murals you've painted. I should have included you, especially since you once said you would help JVS, if needed. You are definitely needed. I need you and Danni both, if possible, at least part of the year. Maybe from March through summer."

Pete glanced at Danni and held his hands out, palms up. "Maybe until you're on your feet. But, that's the high season in Florida. I'll need to fly back and forth. That's when I'll be doing the most art shows."

"That's right. I forgot about that. There's a couple of artsy towns in the Hill Country that you might want to check out for shows during the spring and summertime...even fall."

"Where?"

"Wimberly, for one, though it's a small town, and I don't know how much business you would have. Actually, if you can locate a gallery to show your work in Dallas or Houston, that would probably be your best bet."

"Thanks for letting me know, Vince. I'll need to talk to Danni about this. Could I get back to you later today?"

"Sure, Pete."

***

After they had disconnected, Danni made a new pot of coffee and placed two cranberry orange scones on a plate. After placing the scones and two cups of coffee on the breakfast room table, she and Pete sat down in the comfortable rattan chairs.

"What do you think, darlin'?"

"It would be nice to be away from the summer heat, especially from July through October. I'd be willing to leave in April for this year only. However, in the future, I would rather not leave Florida until the end of June. We could make a couple of weekly trips back and forth. Maybe a trip over New Year's."

"Exactly my feelings."

"It would be nice to be close to Jazzy for a few months out of the year. She could probably locate a cute place for us to live… one with a view and space for an art studio."

"Sounds great to me. Shall I call him back?" Pete asked.

"Sure."

***

Vince clicked his cell phone on, surprised to hear back from Pete so promptly. "Hey, thanks for calling me back so quickly."

"Sure." Pete gave him their decision. Knowing it would not be enough, he said, "I'm sorry, Vince. I know it's not enough. But you will have plenty of help during the summer months. It's November through March that you will be shorthanded. If you can train your office manager to take over during those months, you might consider spending some time down here in Florida."

"As it is, I'm making monthly trips to Florida. I can increase the visits from one weekend to four or five days so that we can, at least, have board meetings there. Sal, Bobby, Danni, if Pete hasn't already been included in our meetings, make sure he is. Is that okay with you, Pete?"

"Sure, Vince. I appreciate it."

"I cannot tell either of you how much I appreciate the time you and Danni are both giving me by spending seven or eight months in Austin this next year. I'll make sure you're both rewarded for it."

"Seeing the Austin operation successful will be reward enough," Danni said.

"Agreed," Pete said. "Especially if I can arrange a few art shows in Austin and paint the Hill Country when the bluebells are in bloom."

CHAPTER 53
CHRISTMAS TIME

On Christmas Eve, Pete, Danni, Bobby, Madison, Vince, Margarite and her father Joseph, Dr. Sam, and his wife Vivian, joined Sal to celebrate Christmas Eve in Sal's new home on the Intracoastal Waterway in Boca Raton. He had purchased a Spanish-style four-bedroom home with a spacious patio overlooking the water, which replaced the luxurious penthouse that he had owned on AIA.

Before dinner was served, during the toasts, Pete stood and said, "To Danni, the most stunning and outstanding woman that I've ever met." Everyone cheered and raised their glasses. "Danni, may I make our announcement?"

She nodded.

"I have to tell all of you that this is the happiest day of my life. When I first set eyes on this gorgeous woman, she took my breath away. I am more than pleased to say that she has agreed to my proposal of marriage."

The applause from everyone present, including Sal, was tremendous.

"When and where is the wedding going to be held?" Madison asked.

"May seventh, at sunset. We would like to have a private

ceremony on the beach in Key West with our best friends attending," Danni said.

Madison glanced down at Danni's left hand. Her eyes twinkled. "Oh my God! You're wearing your engagement ring. It's beautiful."

"It's gorgeous, and I love it. But, I love Pete more, much more, than I could ever say," Danni said, smiling gently at Pete.

"We're going to be such great friends," Madison said. "I could have never wished for a more wonderful cousin-in-law."

"Nor I."

CHAPTER 54
NEW YEARS EVE

On New Year's Eve, Danni, Pete, Madison, Sal, Bobby, Vince, Margarite, and her father, Joseph, met at Jazzy's on 6th for her special performance. Starring with her tonight only was a beautiful woman originally from New Orleans, once known as "The Toast of New Orleans."

When Jazzy invited her to the stage, Danni rose, dressed in a crimson ankle-length skirt with a low-cut top to match, along with a narrow gold belt, gold jewelry, and high-heeled sandals, Pete's mouth dropped open. Vince and Sal glanced at each other with wide grins. Both had known of Danni's secret talents for years. She had performed privately in their homes for special occasions each year for the past twenty years. She'd also performed in private for Pete, but he had no idea she had once been a professional.

The opening set featured Jazzy at the piano, accompanied by her band, with Danni singing "What are you Doing New Year's Eve?" Following the introduction, she performed tunes by Etta Mae James and Billie Holiday, "Born on the Bayou," "Got My Mojo Workin'," "Crawlin' King snake," "Gonna Have Some Fun Tonight," and "Honey, Don't Tear My Clothes."

Thomas and Evelyn, along with Running Deer and Lainey,

entered the club while Danni was singing and dancing to "Born on the Bayou." As they sat at a table near the front that had been reserved for them, Danni didn't see them until she was halfway through the song. She smiled, winked, and moved closer to their table.

During the second set, Jazzy sang and danced to tunes by Etta Mae James, "Gotta Serve Somebody," "Walkin' the Back Streets," Aretha Franklin's "Respect," and "Do Right Woman — Do Right Man" while Danni played the piano. Their final song of the night featured Jazzy, Danni, and her band.

When the performance was over, they left to have a quiet cocktail in the lounge at the Driskill Hotel, where they planned a late-night dinner in Thomas and Evelyn's luxurious king suite.

"You are coming to our wedding, aren't you?"

"We wouldn't miss it. I would like a favor from both you and Jazzy though," Thomas said.

"What's that?"

"We would love for you and Jazzy to perform at our Valentine's Day Special in Las Vegas. Plan on doing a couple of song and dance routines. You're both spectacular. The audience in Vegas will love you."

Evelyn's eyes sparkled. "You must. Both of you are so talented. Chrissie will adore being with you!"

"You're serious, aren't you?" Danni asked.

"Yes, we're serious."

"Pete, how do you feel about this?"

"Darlin' I'd love it. You're far too talented not to accept. Besides, it will be fun."

"Jazzy?"

"Are you kidding? I wouldn't miss it."

"Then it's settled. You are all invited. We're hoping that Evelyn's parents, Katherine and William, will be able to make it, too."

"We'll plan on it."

CHAPTER 55
VALENTINE'S DAY

On February twelfth, Vince arrived at the Boca Raton Airport in the company's private plane. Madison and Elizabeth were waiting at the airport for him when he arrived.

"Thanks for picking me up, Madison." He caught her in his arms and hugged her, kissing her lightly on her cheek.

"You're welcome. I've missed you."

Vince's eyes lit up. "You have? Really?"

"Yes, really."

"Well, that's good news. I've missed little Elizabeth, too. She is such a sweet little baby."

"She's also a happy baby. She never cries. And now that she is nine months old, I'm taking her to swimming lessons."

"At her age?" Vince asked.

Madison laughed. "Yes. It's a class just for babies her age. She has a lesson this afternoon after her nap. Would you like to come with us?"

"I sure would. Will you pick me up at Bobby's?"

"Better yet, I'd like you to stay with us."

Vince's face lit up. His mouth split into a wide grin. "Do you mean it?"

"Of course I do. I want you to have the opportunity of playing

253

with Elizabeth, feeding her, and bathing her. You are her father, after all."

"I don't know what to say."

"It's time that you became acquainted with her."

***

That evening, after he and Madison had put Elizabeth to bed, Madison said, "You can put your suitcase in my room, Vince. You don't need to sleep in the guest room."

"Do you mean…?"

She nodded. "It's been far too long. I've loved you from the first time I saw you, and after becoming better acquainted with who you are now, I love you even more. I won't keep you waiting any longer."

"I'm speechless," he said, taking her in his arms. "Does this mean that you will marry me?"

"Yes."

"Sunday? In Las Vegas, with all of our friends there?"

"Yes"

"I don't have your ring with me."

"I just want you, Vince. The ring's beautiful, but I don't need one."

"You're amazing, Madison. You can't imagine how happy this makes me."

***

On the thirteenth of February, during cocktail hour at Thomas's house with all of their friends gathered around, including the children and Baby Elizabeth, Vince stood to make an announcement. "I have an announcement to make, and an invitation to extend to all of you. Madison has finally accepted my proposal of marriage. We have our marriage license and will be married on February fifteenth at six p.m. Thomas and Evelyn have been so gracious and have insisted upon a garden wedding, here in his home. Since Madison is a Methodist, she has asked that Reverend Carson of the Methodist Church here in Las Vegas conduct the ceremony."

"You are all invited," Thomas said, standing. He lifted his glass of champagne and said, "A toast to Madison and Vince. Wishing you happiness always and a long life together."

Everyone applauded and wished them well. Elizabeth awoke and began speaking in her own baby language. The only thing anyone understood was "mama." She sat up, smiled, waved to her audience, and clapped her hands.

"A natural-born actress," Thomas said. "She loves the attention."

"Chrissie," Julie said, "Elizabeth just may be joining us on stage one day."

***

The following evening, February fourteenth, Chrissie's nanny took care of Elizabeth while all of the adults joined Thomas and Evelyn at their Valentine's Day Special. Just as they had done four years ago on New Year's Eve, Thomas and Julie thrilled the audience with their performances. Chrissie and Julie had worked up a more complicated routine, which the audience adored. Chrissie, at the young age of nine-years old, was well on her way to becoming a beloved entertainer, just as her father was.

After Chrissie and Julie's performance, Thomas took the microphone and announced a guest performance by Austin's own Jazzy Boudreaux & her New Orleans band, along with Danni Giardini, once known as The Toast of New Orleans. They chose hot blues and jazz songs by Etta James, Billie Holiday, and Aretha Franklin that they often performed at various clubs on Sixth Street in Austin.

After an encore, there was a standing ovation.

***

255

On February fifteenth, Madison and Vince were married with their friends present. It was a beautiful evening and a wonderful ceremony. Baby Elizabeth was present at her parents' wedding, accompanied by her new friend Chrissie and the adults. After the ceremony, Elizabeth clapped and smiled with the rest of the wedding party.

EPILOGUE

May seventh at sunset, on the beach in Key West, just as the sun met the horizon in a brilliant flash of green, Pete and Danni were married. The vows that they had so carefully written bound them together during this lifetime. After they had dined with their friends, they boarded a sailboat chartered for the Virgin Islands.

***

When Pete and Danni departed, Sal took the only opportunity he'd had that evening to speak with Vince privately. "Great wedding, wasn't it?"

"Wonderful. It's been obvious for months that they are very much in love," Vince said. "I'm happy for them."

"Is Margarite seeing anyone?"

Vince chuckled. "So you're interested in Margarite?"

"I have been for months."

"Then why don't you ask her to dinner? Or to a live performance? I know for a fact that she's interested in you."

"Why didn't you tell me?"

Vince's mouth split into a wide grin. "You never have had a problem with women before. I figured if you were really interested in Margarite, you would get around to it."

"She's very pretty; seems nice, too."

"She is about the sweetest girl that I've ever met. Her father saved my life."

"What do you mean?"

"She and her father were driving through the Taos pass when the shuttle that I was riding in went off the cliff. Her father stopped, called 911, and hiked down the mountain to where the shuttle had landed. Joseph, God bless him, pulled me out of the shuttle and carried me to safety. We barely made it before the vehicle exploded."

"My God, Vince. You owe your life to him."

"He and his daughter, Margarite, visited me often in the hospital. They took me home with them once I was released."

"What wonderful people," Sal said. "I think I would really like Margarite. She's different, just as Danni and Madison are. So, do you think she's interested in me?"

"I do. Better hurry up before someone else finds her. Come to Austin soon. Stay with Madison and me if you want to."

"Thanks, Vince. I think everything's going to work out, and I'm so glad to have you back, partner."

Vince chuckled. *Good to have you back too. It won't be long before you're living in Austin full time.*

***

Nearing midnight, Pete and Danni sat on the deck sipping glasses of champagne under a full moon, with stars sparkling like miniature diamonds against a midnight blue sky.

"This is a dream come true. After all that we have been through over the past year, it seems as though fate brought us together."

The corners of Pete's mouth tipped up. "I have known since I first set eyes on you in the library of the Grand Duchess Hotel that you were my destiny, darlin."

"And you mine."

The End

Weslynn McCallister, pseudonym, Jamie Cortland was born in Evansville, Indiana and raised in Roswell, New Mexico. A published novelist and an award-winning poet, she is a member of Sisters in Crime, the Mystery Writers of America, and is a founding member of the Florida Writers Association.

Educated in the fine arts, she has worked as a high fashion model, graphic designer, and as a real estate agent. Her hobby is ballroom dancing. Today, she lives in southwest Florida near the Gulf of Mexico.